LP

Southard - A reckoning at Arrowhead

DEC 0 1 1990

Yours to Keep
Withdrawn/ABCL

A Reckoning at Arrowhead

Also available in Large Print
by W. W. Southard:

Season of Vengeance

A Reckoning at Arrowhead

W. W. Southard

G.K.HALL &CO.
Boston, Massachusetts
1985

Copyright © 1983 by W. W. Southard.

All rights reserved.

Published in Large Print by arrangement with Bantam Books, Inc.

G. K. Hall Large Print Book Series.

Set in 18 pt Times Roman.

Library of Congress Cataloging in Publication Data

Southard, W. W.
  A reckoning at Arrowhead.

  (G.K. Hall large print book series)
  "Published in large print by arrangement with Bantam Books, Inc."—Verso of t.p.
  1. Large type books.   I. Title.   II. Series.
[PS3569.O763R44   1985]   813'.54   85-8733
ISBN 0-8161-3800-1 (lg. print)

*To my children
Greg, Pam, and Brette*

A Reckoning at Arrowhead

1

They say you never hear the bullet that has your name on it, but Blondy Kincaid wasn't so lucky.

The sound of the shot that snatched him from the saddle rose out of the rocky canyon walls like a peal of thunder announcing the end of the world. His ears continued to ring even after the bright light of midday faded to a smoky gray and flickered out altogether.

At the instant it happened, the palomino stallion was halfway across the Piedra River and liking the icy water less at every step. The river was roiling and muddy and high, swollen by the runoff from a hard winter's snow high in the San Cristobal Mountains.

It was the stallion's reluctance that saved Blondy's life, although he didn't know it. A swooping current of chill water washed into the crevice between the animal's powerful thighs and caused him to hesitate the tenth part of a second, reconsidering this foolishness his master was demanding of him. That was the needle point in time when a finger tightened on the trigger of a .44-caliber Henry and sent three grains of lead toward the sweat-stained hat of Blondy Kincaid.

A man shooting downhill tends to overshoot his target unless he takes deliberate cognizance of the angle. This particular gunman was well aware of that law of trajectory, but he didn't foresee the stallion's hesitation. So the bullet, instead of mushrooming inside the rider's skull, carved a furrow in the bright blond hair, flattened itself against his shoulder blade, and caromed away into the torrent slashing angrily along the riverbed.

Blondy muttered, "Aw, hell," as a matter of reflex, and pitched sideways into the churning stream. After that his mind wandered without direction, jolting him back in time to a dingy tavern in the border town of Juarez and a raven-haired señorita who pulled at his golden hair and cackled in his ear until his head was fit to burst.

He tasted gunmetal and muddy water and smiled grimly at the certain knowledge his time had come.

High on the side of the canyon wall, behind a fortress of lichen-carpeted boulders, two men watched. One leaned with his elbows hooked across the crown of a great stone and peered through the buckhorn sights of the Henry rifle at the figure floating far below.

"You suppose I ought to put another one in him?"

His partner scratched in preoccupation at the point where his beard was prickling the tender flesh of his neck and grunted with casual interest.

"Don't matter much. He's dead twice over, what with that slug between his ears and inhalin' a few gallons of Piedra River water."

The bearded man turned and started toward the copse of cedar trees where two saddle horses stood ground-tied.

"Let's go down and take a look," he said. "Shore wouldn't want that palomino horse to wander off. I'm staking my claim on him right now."

A momentary frown touched the rifleman's face. Then he eased the hammer down on the scarred Henry repeater and trailed after his companion.

Not far from where the rider had fallen into the water, the stream took a sudden and precipitous turn, dashing itself into frothy madness against a gravel bank before plunging on down the canyon. Toward that sloping bank shot the limp form of Blondy Kincaid, and a moment later, like a beached canoe, he had been thrust onto the gravel bar.

It took the two horsemen the better part of a half-hour to thread their way through the sloping forest of boulders to the canyon floor. At last they drew rein on a grassy shelf beside the rushing stream.

The one who had pulled the trigger on the rifle dismounted, hunkered down with his back to a boulder, and began to roll a cigarette. One eye watched the making of the smoke while the other appeared to be straying downriver. That was how he had come by the nickname of Skew Eye. More than one adversary had learned the painful lesson that the misaligned eyes had no effect whatever on his ability to aim a gun.

Now he said smugly, "That's a fair piece of shootin', if I do say so. Must be a good three hundred yards."

Nabours, his companion, still sat his saddle.

"Yeah, real tough shot. Sorta like shooting fish in a barrel." He pulled his horse around. "I'm going to catch that claybank horse this jasper was riding before he gets plum to Mexico."

Skew Eye was finishing his second cigarette when the bearded man returned with the gold-hued horse trailing behind. He had been thinking about his partner and the palomino during that interval, and when he spoke again there was resentment in his tone.

"How come you get the horse and I don't get nothin'?" he demanded.

Nabours spat a long stream of tobacco juice into the fringe of dirty foam that laced the edge of the river.

"Because I say so. That's why." He stepped down from his horse. "I'll tell you what, though. You can have anything you find on the body. Except his gun. I'm takin' that."

Skew shook his head, frowning at the complexity of the circumstances.

"Now, dammit, Luke. That ain't right." It was the whine of a man who didn't really expect fairness, from his companion or from life.

Nabours ignored the plaintive observation and tossed the reins of the two horses to the other.

"I'm gonna have me that ivory-handled Colt's and that fancy gunbelt that hombre is wearin'. Hope to hell the water hasn't ruint it."

He skirted a jagged boulder at the water's

edge and stepped onto the gravel bank where the limp form of the rider was sprawled, the blood from his wounds turning the muddy flood waters a deeper, darker red.

Nabours caught a handful of shirt and pulled. The body resisted stubbornly.

"Give me a hand. He's a damn sight heavier than he looks."

Skew moved to the water's edge and grasped a limp arm. Between them they dragged the body to a level patch of ground and dropped the man on his back. Nabours sank to one knee, unbuckled the heavy, embossed gunbelt, and pulled it from Kincaid's waist.

"Nice, huh?" he mumbled, not bothering to look up at Skew's disgruntled countenance. "I'll bet you six bits he stoled it."

Skew made a quick search of Blondy's pockets and swore in disgust.

A handful of change and a pocketknife were his only reward. He put a booted foot against Kincaid's hip, preparing to roll the lifeless form back into the plunging stream, when his eye fell on the belt about his victim's waist. Its thickness was extraordinary.

Skew knelt and unfastened the heavy silver buckle. Nabours, examining the .45-caliber Colt Peacemaker, failed to notice.

His brow wrinkling in concentration, Skew unlaced the upper edge of the wide belt. A thick, tight mass of bills stared up at him. He sucked in his breath and drew Nabours' attention.

"What's that you got?" the bearded man demanded.

"Nothin'. Just a belt," Skew said defensively.

"Nothin', hell! Let me look at that!"

Skew drew back, holding the money belt against his chest.

"You said I could have whatever I found on him. You got his horse and his gun."

Nabours' hands were drawn into tight fists. His eyes were cold. A half-minute passed while he glared at Skew's sweat-beaded face. At last Nabours relaxed and put a hand on the smaller man's shoulder.

"Hey, we're partners, ain't we? I was fixin' to tell you you could have my old gun and gunbelt. Now, let's see what you've got there."

When Skew still refused, Nabours reached out with a long arm and snatched the belt from his hands. The ivory-handled gun and gunbelt forgotten, he began to pull the sheaf of bills from the money belt. He placed them in careful, moist rows on the flattened crown of the boulder, swearing under his breath at each new pile.

Silently Skew Eye watched the process, one booted foot still in the water and his mouth slackly open.

At last the bearded cowboy stepped back, hooked his thumbs in his belt, and grinned until his eyes were all but hidden behind the slitted lids.

"Ain't it the damnedest thing you ever seen? I mean, who would have figured it? There must be a thousand dollars right there on that rock."

Suddenly he turned his eyes on his companion. The grin had a different look.

"Tell you what, Skew. It ain't fair for me to take his gun. You go ahead and have it. And that fine Mex'can gunbelt. Why, I imagine they cost better'n a hundred."

"Now, dammit, Luke! You ain't takin' all that money. I found it. And you said . . ."

Luke had unbuttoned his shirt across his lean belly and was stuffing the bills inside with quick motions.

"There ain't near as much as I thought. Not more'n three or four hundred. It probably looked like more because it's wet." He buttoned his shirt. "Now, you go ahead and strap on that jasper's gunbelt. He won't be needin' that fancy six-gun no more."

There was a look of bottled-up rage in the eye of Skew, a look that only a longtime acquaintance would perceive. Nabours read the look and knew he had pushed the slow-witted man too far.

The tense silence was shattered by a moan. Both men jerked about in startled wonder and stared down at the sodden figure on the ground. His head rolled to one side and a geyser of water erupted from his throat.

The next instant Nabours was grinning again.

"Dang me if he ain't still alive. Tell you what, Skew. There ain't no doubt but what the law's on his trail. Anybody with a lick of sense can see that. Let's haul him back to the ranch and send word to the sheriff. And you can have every cent of the reward!"

Skew considered the words for a long moment, then broke into an uncertain smile. Maybe Luke wasn't trying to sucker him, after all.

Nabours drew a sack of tobacco from his pocket.

"Might as well wait a few minutes. I don't particularly hanker to carry him if he can walk." He settled against the boulder and rolled himself a cigarette, watching beneath the brim of his hat the face of his companion. Skew's temper was volatile, and impossible of prediction.

But Skew had forgotten his earlier displeasure.

"He sure takes a heap of killin'," he said. "Reminds me of a lobo wolf I shot oncet. Blew half his head away, and that critter still got up and drug hisself off into the trees. I tracked him for two mile before I lost him. It was plumb spooky."

Nabours reached out with a toe and rolled Kincaid onto his side. Another groan issued from the wounded man's throat.

"Maybe I ought to cave in his skull," Luke muttered, hefting a river-smoothed stone twice the size of his fist.

"Hey, I thought we were going to take him in and collect the reward," Skew protested.

"Yeah, sure. If Old Man Grimm don't cross us up. He's bad enough anytime, but he's hell to deal with where money's concerned."

"Well, I ain't giving up the reward to nobody," Skew said angrily. "It was me that done the shootin', and I'm takin' the money. Grimm can kiss my behind."

Nabours decided against reminding the skew-eyed cowboy that the reward was something less than a gold-plated certainty. He would cross that bridge when he had to. He slid the money belt, now devoid of its contents, back around the wounded man's waist.

They lapsed into silence, watching with no sign of emotion as the slender, sodden man on the ground began to stir. Blood was still oozing through the golden mat of hair and running in rivulets across his cheek. His right shoulder was caked with drying blood, already turning from deep crimson to a crusted blackness.

At last, using one arm with painful awkwardness, Kincaid rose to a sitting position, and immediately vomited up great quantities of water. After a time he propped himself up against a huge stone and sat there limply, panting with the exertion.

Still the two cowboys were silent. They could have been watching the throes of a dying fish for all the compassion that showed in their faces.

After a time Kincaid nodded toward the breast of Skew, where a round paper tag hung by a yellow string from a shirt pocket.

"A smoke sure would go good," Blondy said.

Skew glanced toward Nabours, who inclined his head in a brief nod. Skew Eye drew the sack from his pocket and tossed it to the ground beside the wounded man. Slowly, his numbed right arm propped across one knee, Kincaid rolled the cigarette, then looked toward Luke Nabours.

"My matches must have got wet, too."

Nabours nodded again, and Skew reached over to light the cigarette. Blondy drew in a lungful of smoke, then watched the exhaled wisp of gray float toward the pure blue of the noonday sky above.

"Who do I have to thank for the welcome?" he asked blandly.

Skew grinned, one eye on Blondy's face and the other wandering among the treetops.

"Why, I guess that'd be me," he said. "You oughta be dead. I don't usually miss."

"You always greet strangers like this?" Blondy asked.

Nabours swore dispassionately.

"When they're on Old Man Grimm's place we do. You're luckier than most."

Grimm! The name flashed like a bolt of nighttime lightning across Blondy's mind. He grinned a tight smile to hide his thoughts.

"This Grimm feller don't take too kindly to visitors, I take it."

"You take it right," the bearded man grunted. "And you're fixin' to get a chance to find out just how keerect you are. That's where we're headed right now."

Nabours and Skew mounted their horses and sat silently, watching the wounded man struggle into his saddle. When they moved out, following the game trail that paralleled the river, Nabours was in the lead and Skew was trailing behind. Between them rode Blondy, the reins hanging loose across the palomino's neck. The pain in his head and shoulder was his whole world. Consciousness came and went. Someone had a branding iron, fresh from the coals of a cow-chip fire, pressed against his flesh. He wondered fretfully what brand they were putting on him.

He came to his senses once, and that was a mistake. He opened his eyes and watched the sky and the earth swap places, and fell head down to the water-worn rocks beside the trail. Skew helped him back onto his horse, and they rode on. Only an instinctive balance drawn from a lifetime in the saddle kept him astride the stallion.

During a lucid few moments he remembered what he had been about before the bullet had jerked him from the saddle, and that remembrance kindled a new surge of agony in his brain. Now the Colonel would know for certain that Blondy Kincaid was a no-account drifter who ought to have been left right there in jail.

He tried to picture the face of Colonel Webster Buchanan. It was something to do between periods of unconsciousness. He kept seeing the Colonel in his wheelchair, his face the chiseled countenance of a bald eagle, bushy white brows overhanging the eyes of a meat-eater. And Blondy had about as much chance of escaping the reach of Colonel Webster Buchanan as did a field mouse fleeing the talons of an eagle. If he'd had half the sense God gave a goose, he'd have stayed in jail and told the Colonel to take a long walk.

Kincaid gave it up, and slid sideways from the saddle. But this time Skew was there to catch him. They rode up to the ranch house that way, Blondy out cold and half-lying across the neck of Skew's horse. He didn't even feel it when Skew turned him loose and let him fall.

It wasn't a particularly noteworthy sight that Blondy missed. Orlando Grimm's ranch house wasn't much to look at from the outside. It had started as a two-room shack; then a room had been added here, another there, until the original structure had lost its identity. A wall of honeysuckle vines, home for an ancient mongrel dog, served as a fence across the front of the house. A hitch rail, worn to a gloss by the rubbing of countless horses, anchored one end of the flagstone path to the front door. Beyond stood a half-dozen barns and sheds, all in the same state of weathered exhaustion. Among them wandered a motley tribe of chickens in eternal quest of invisible morsels.

Nabours got down, glanced at the lifeless form of the man on the ground, and walked on toward the house.

Skew yelled, "Hey, Luke. Give me a hand. This feller weighs a ton."

Nabours didn't even look back.

Skew had Blondy by one arm, backing toward the walk. When he saw that Nabours was not going to help, he dropped the wounded man in the dust and hurried on to the house. He had an investment to protect.

Nabours was doing fine until he crossed the open veranda and reached for the knob of the heavy wooden door. At that point he slowed, took his hat from his head, and reached out to knock decorously. No need to antagonize the old man any more than necessary. The crazy old coot could fly off the handle and make a man hanker to be someplace else. He had a tongue that could skin a hog without it being scalded.

A girl opened the door, a girl who wore short hair and jeans that buttoned down the front because she didn't especially want to look like a girl. The bulge, slight though it was, in the front of the man's shirt she wore made Nabours' breath quicken, as it always did. The voice that bellowed from the vicinity of the dining table made him forget it—fast.

"What the hell you boys doin' here? This ain't no Fourth of July holiday. You and Skew was sent to ride the river for strays. Did you forget, or was it that you couldn't find the river?"

Nabours wanted to stride across the room and belt the old man in the mouth. My, how he wanted to. Instead, he backed up a step and put on a half-smile.

"We ran into somethin' we figured you'd want to know about, Mr. Grimm. We was ridin' the river breaks like you wanted, when—"

Orlando Grimm shoved his dinner plate away in a crash of china and silverware. He stood up to better broadcast his rage, but the standing up didn't help much. He wasn't tall enough to be impressive. The voice that boomed from his barrel chest, however, more than made up for other inadequacies.

"The only thing I want to know about is them steers you so-called cowboys let get by you yesterday. I swear, a ten-year-old kid would be worth more to me than you and that gotch-eyed sidekick of yours."

The veins were standing out in bold relief on Grimm's forehead. Nabours took a deep breath and bowed his neck.

"A cow thief! That's what we come on down in the canyon." He paused an instant, watching the magical effect of the words. "This jasper had one of your yearlin' heifers down and was heatin' up a runnin' iron. We got him before he could burn a hair on that critter's hide, though."

"A rustler!" The word exploded from Grimm's throat like a taut wire breaking.

"Sure as sunup," Nabours hurried on. "We spotted his fire and snuck up to the lip of the canyon. He must have heard us, 'cause he went for his shootin' iron. Got off a half-dozen shots before we could draw a bead on him."

"Did you shoot him?" The girl still stood with her hand on the knob of the door.

"Yeah. We wanted to wing him, but it

was him or us."

"Did you get him buried?" Grimm demanded.

"Naw," said Nabours. "Not yet. We tried to keep him alive, but he was hit pretty bad. We brung him along to the house, but it ain't likely he's still breathin'."

He turned as a shadow fell across the door. Skew was standing there with his face screwed into a deep frown. He wasn't sure what story Luke Nabours had told, but he was quite certain it was something other than the precise truth.

"Ain't that right, Skew?" Nabours demanded. "He tried to gun us when we caught him with that yearlin'."

"Yeah, sure. That's a fact, Mr. Grimm. He was fixin' to kill that critter and carve hisself a steak when we seen him."

Grimm's head swiveled about on its short, thick neck. Nabours shifted his feet.

"It was a long ways," he said quickly. "You know ol' Skew can't see so good at a distance."

"Let's go take a look," the rancher said.

Blondy still lay where Skew had dropped him. He was on his stomach in the powdery soil, a black circle of drying blood swelling out from his shoulder.

Grimm rolled him half over with the toe of a boot and studied the ashen face.

"Never seen him before. Must be a drifter. A lone rider."

"That's what we figured," Skew said. "He's bound to be runnin' from the law. Hell's bells. We found—"

Nabours spun quickly around. The rowel of his big Spanish spur raked a deep furrow across Skew's shin. The latter swore heatedly, drawing a damning look from Grimm. But the girl wasn't listening. Abruptly she bent down.

"He's still alive!"

She pointed to the ground an inch in front of Blondy's nose. Intermittently, a tiny jet of dust erupted from the soil.

"He's breathin', all right," said Orlando Grimm. "Too bad. Looks like we'll have us a hangin', after all."

The girl looked up.

"He needs doctoring, Dad. We can't just let him lie there."

Grimm scowled.

"Now, Dru Lee, don't you go frettin' yourself about this polecat. There ain't but one thing to do with a rustler. Don't matter if he's half-alive or half-dead."

He turned to Nabours.

"Put him on his horse and lead him over to that cottonwood tree." He fixed the girl with a paternal look. "You run along back to the house, girl. Ain't somethin' you ought to be seein'."

It took both Nabours and Skew to wrestle the limp form into the saddle on the palomino. Lightning bolts of pain lancing through his shoulder cleared the haze from Blondy's mind. Clinging precariously to the saddle horn, he opened his eyes and squinted at the burly rancher. When he spoke, the words ran together like those of a drunk.

"Where the hell am I?"

"You're on my spread, young feller. The Rafter G. I'm Orlando Grimm. And that was a Rafter G critter you was fixin' to put a brand on."

Kincaid knew the old man's words had some special significance, but it didn't seem worth the effort to pursue it.

"I hate to be a bother," he muttered, "but I sure could use some help getting down from this horse."

Grimm's scowl deepened.

"Appears you don't savvy the trouble you're in, friend. In this part of the country we don't take too kindly to cow stealin'. Now, you just hang on to that saddle horn a couple more minutes and all your troubles will be over."

Kincaid's mind was clearing. The sound of the rancher's words had a splendidly illuminating effect. He looked at the rope in Nabours' hand and back to the old man.

"If it wouldn't put you out any, I'd appreciate an explanation. Who says I'm a cow thief?"

"Both of these boys saw you with a Rafter G heifer down in the river canyon. Why don't you tell me who you're ridin' for before we have to knot up this perfectly good rope. Are you one of Slick Detwiler's hands?"

"Never heard the name."

"Okay, boys," said Grimm. "Take him to the tree."

2

Kincaid's thoughts were speeding at an aching, frantic pace through his head.

"How much you figure that heifer was worth?"

The question stopped the rancher in mid-stride. It was a topic that monopolized his thoughts from the moment he awoke in the morning until sleep closed the subject at night. Any reference to money drew Orlando Grimm like a moth to a coal-oil lamp.

"Why, a heifer that's nearly full-growed is easy worth"—he couldn't resist adding five dollars to what he knew was the top market price—"twenty-five dollars. Rafter G stock is as good as any you'll find anywhere in the territory."

"I'll pay you four times the price of that critter if you'll throw in an hour of time and a last meal."

Grimm grinned without humor.

"I ain't never seen a drifter yet that had two coins to rub together. How do you figure on coming up with a hundred dollars?"

Skew's head had snapped around and now he was looking wildly at Nabours. It was painfully obvious where this line of talk was heading.

"Do we have a deal?" Blondy asked.

Nabours handed Skew the reins of the stallion and hurried back to stand in front of Grimm.

"He's feedin' you a line of bull, boss. We searched him after he was down. To make sure he didn't have no other gun. And there wasn't a *centavo* on him anywhere." Nabours' voice was agitated. "Let's get it over with."

"Shut your face, Luke," Grimm snapped. "I want to hear what this young feller has to say. Okay, boy. You've got yourself a deal." He glanced upward, gauging the angle of the sun. "Won't hurt nothing to give you another hour."

He turned and started toward the house.

"Take him inside, boys. And there ain't no need to drag him around like you was fixin' to cut a dogie calf. Be easy."

Nabours gave Skew a look that placed all the blame for the unfortunate turn of events squarely on the man with the misaligned eyes. Skew opened his mouth to protest, but Luke broke in.

"You take his hoss to the corral. I'll manage him."

He grasped Blondy by his right arm and gave a sharp jerk. Kincaid's reaction was instinctive. He let out a yelp that stopped Grimm in the act of reaching for the knob of the door. Deliberately the rancher strode back to Nabours.

That puncher, although a head taller than Grimm, turned a shade pale and backed against the horse. Grimm's left hand shot out and grabbed a handful of his shirt, while his right moved in a blur against the cowboy's bearded face. Nabours' head rocked back with the force of the slap. His right hand dropped to the worn butt of the .44 Colt low on his right hip.

If Grimm saw the move, he ignored it.

"You don't hear so good, do you, Luke? I've noticed it before. You can't seem to recollect who bosses this spread."

The rancher stepped back.

"Now pick him up and help him inside. Just like he was a newborn baby. You savvy?"

Nabours nodded, but his eyes burned with

sulfuric fire beneath his heavy brows.

Blondy could feel the warmth of new blood from the freshly opened wound coursing down his side. With Luke under his left arm he walked toward the house, his legs threatening to give way at each step.

The girl had stopped in the midst of clearing the dinner table to put down a clean plate. Beside it was a platter of thick steaks, sourdough biscuits, gravy, red beans flecked with fiery-hot chili peppers, and a mug of thick black coffee. Suddenly Kincaid couldn't tell the pain in his shoulder from the pangs of hunger.

The girl pulled the chair out but shrank back as though she were afraid of touching the wounded man. As he slid into the chair, though, his shoulder brushed her hand. She jerked it away and stared down at the smear of bright new blood across her knuckles. There was the faintest hint of a tremor in her voice.

"He needs tending to, Dad."

Grimm had straddled a chair backwards and was tamping tobacco in a corncob pipe.

"Now, you just go on in the kitchen and let him eat, Dru Lee."

Nabours chuckled.

"He ain't gonna have time to heal, nohow."

Grimm, poised to strike a match on the heavy silver buckle at his waist, stopped abruptly and fixed Nabours with a flinty glare.

"Dru Lee. You fetch some rags and wrap up that shoulder of his'n. We made a deal. This boy's got hisself an hour, and I aim to see he lives to the end of it."

Blondy watched in fascination as the girl gently removed his shirt and began to bathe the angry crimson-rimmed slash in his shoulder. Her hands were soft and smooth, not the rough, callused, ranch-hardened hands he had expected.

"You're lucky," she told him. "The bullet hit a bone and turned out."

He looked into her clear hazel eyes and had the strange feeling he had seen those eyes somewhere before.

"Yeah, terrible lucky," he grunted. "If that bullet had of killed me, your dad would've been cheated out of all his fun."

Her gentle touch turned suddenly severe, and he had to grit his teeth. Forcing his mind to shut out the pain, he let his thoughts wander about the big room, inventorying its details: the scarred oak dining table that had sat in one spot so long its legs had dented the wooden floor; a huge fireplace crudely fashioned of native stones; on the wall above it, the sweeping antlers of a mule deer buck, serving as a rack for the long-barreled repeating rifle, its stock chipped and battered and the barrel worn shiny with use. A big .56-caliber Spencer, big enough for bear or buffalo, Blondy deduced, then whimpered aloud as the girl doused the wound with turpentine.

Tearing a bed sheet into strips, she bound his right shoulder tightly and expertly. Only then did it occur to him that some luck remained to him. Had it been his left hand, he would have been all but helpless for using a gun or a rope. Supposing he ever again had a chance to use either.

When she had finished, Kincaid one-handedly attacked the plate of food. He had had a cigarette for breakfast, and nothing since. He became aware that she had sat down across the table from him and was watching him eat. Once he thought he saw a smile start on her lips, then fade. She had short hair that was no particular shade of brown, and a band of freckles across her nose. Well, she wasn't beautiful, Blondy told himself, and tried to concentrate on his eating. But he found himself wanting to look again into those deep hazel eyes.

Abruptly Orlando Grimm stood up and slid a worn gold timepiece from his vest pocket.

"That's your hour and some change, young feller. We made a deal. You recollect?"

Kincaid nodded.

"I'm going to add another twenty for the meal. I've never eaten better."

The rancher's eyebrows went up. He wasn't really convinced this skinny cow thief could muster twenty cents, much less a hundred and twenty dollars. But the prospect caused him to lick his lower lip.

Careful to keep his wounded shoulder immobile, Blondy began to unbuckle his belt. Skew appeared suddenly in the open door. When his good eye grasped the state of affairs, he sucked in a lungful of air. Nabours turned a look on his companion that would have ignited a fire in a green cow chip.

Blondy held the belt out toward the girl.

"I'd be obliged if you'd unlace it, ma'am."

She took the belt and began to work the leather lacing loose. The three men stood rooted where they were, Grimm still astraddle his chair at the head of the table and the two cowpunchers shoulder-to-shoulder just inside the door. Grimm's expression was vulturelike. Nabours' was that of a man taken suddenly ill with an intestinal complaint.

Blondy had his eyes on Orlando Grimm.

"Just take it all out and lay it on the table," he said to Dru Lee. "It needs to dry anyway."

The silence that followed his words was interminable. At last he turned and looked at her.

"It's empty," she said tonelessly. "There's not any money. There's not anything in it."

Blondy took a long, quick step and snatched the belt from her hands. Then he pivoted about to face Nabours and Skew Eye.

"You boys wouldn't happen to know where the money in that belt disappeared to, would you? It was there when I went into the river."

Skew had his mouth open to speak, but Nabours cut him off.

"You claimin' we stole some money from you? You're full of horse manure, fella." He turned to Grimm. "It's hot air he's talkin'. Just trying to put off the necktie party."

The look on Orlando Grimm's face was a study in contradictions. He knew the kind of man this drifter was. Never in his life would he have more than a single month's wages in his pockets at one time. Yet his declaration carried the ring of truth.

"How much money you talkin' about?" he demanded.

"A thousand dollars. Gold certificates. In twenties and fifties."

"A thousand dollars!" Grimm rolled his eyes upward. "If you was aimin' to convince me you was carrying money, you blew your chances right then. A thousand dollars? Hah!"

He got to his feet and knocked the ashes from his pipe into Blondy's empty plate.

"Time to go, young feller. You've had your hour, a good meal, and a bit of a laugh at my expense. I'll take your horse and call it square. You won't be needin' him anymore."

Skew's brows were drawn into a deep, troubled frown. There was something he had to know. He spoke before Nabours could silence him.

"Before we stretch your neck, hombre, how much money does the law have on your scalp?"

"What is that supposed to mean?" Grimm growled.

"Well," said Skew, "me and Luke was talkin'. We figured he had to be on the run."

Nabours had Skew by the arm and was backing toward the door. Grimm stopped them with a quick jerk of his heavy hand.

"How come you two figure that?"

Nabours tightened his grip on Skew's arm until his knuckles turned white. He was muttering under his breath, something the others couldn't hear. He almost made it outside.

"Jest a damned minute!" barked Grimm. "I want to hear the rest of it."

"Nothin', boss. He didn't mean nothin'."

"You shut your face, Luke," the rancher commanded. "Skew can do his own talkin'."

For half a moment Nabours was tempted to ignore Grimm's order, but his resolve melted before he could take another step. They both turned in the doorway.

"Out with it, Skew. What the hell you tryin' to say?"

Skew saw that he was cornered, and he wasn't quite sure why. But his fear of Luke's bullying was several degrees less than his dread of Orlando Grimm's temper.

"Well, we figured since he was so well-heeled he had to be runnin' from the law. Luke promised me I could have the reward."

Grimm's face was cast in granite.

"What do you mean, 'well-heeled'?"

Nabours couldn't help himself.

"He means the gun and gunbelt he was wearin', boss. Mighty fancy iron. Yessirree. Ain't that so, Skew?"

Skew muttered, "Well, yeah," but his head was swiveling back and forth on his neck. The conversation had outdistanced him.

Without taking his eyes from Skew, Grimm very carefully placed his corncob pipe on the table, rose, and moved with bowlegged strides to where the cowboy stood frozen.

His voice was ominously gentle.

"Now, you just spit it out. And if you don't tell it straight the first time, I'll wring your neck like a fryin'-size pullet. Did you find any money atall on this here hombre after you shot him out of the saddle?"

Skew's Adam's apple darted frantically up and down his scrawny neck, like a mouse caught in a flour sack. He looked at Nabours, a look of desperate pleading.

"Well, I guess so," he murmured. "We found some. In that belt of his'n."

"How much?"

"Luke said it wasn't more'n three or four hundred. I was to get the reward. . . ."

Grimm pivoted about so quickly Nabours fell back against the door facing. The rancher's big callused hand slapped him once, twice, three times, snapping his head from side to side like a leaf blown by the wind.

"I warned you, Luke. I warned you aplenty. Any man that draws Rafter G pay don't have no secrets from Orlando Grimm. Now, where's the money?"

Nabours' face was no longer fearful. The hard hand of the rancher had erased his apprehension. His slate-gray eyes burned with venom.

"You've done that for the last time, old man."

"Bring me the money and get the hell off my ranch," Grimm barked. "You don't deserve no notice. And you don't get a dime's worth of pay. That goes for both of you no-account jackasses."

Grimm's face was livid with rage. A network of veins bulged across his forehead. His right hand was balled into a fist, but Nabours didn't wait to see what he intended.

"Skew!" His voice shot upward to a scream. "Shoot the old bastard! Shoot 'im!"

Skew had watched the confrontation with growing alarm. His head was suddenly exploding with pain. He felt like throwing up. Luke's command was a cold wind slapping him in the face. Here was a thing to do, a physical act to relieve the tempest inside his skull.

He drew and fired.

Blondy had read the look in Nabours' eyes, even if Orlando Grimm hadn't. He had seen the fear give way to foolhardiness and he knew the cowboy had passed the point of caution. It was a look Kincaid had seen in more than one man's eyes a fragment of a second before his own Colt had bucked in his hand.

When Nabours barked his command to Skew, Blondy's left hand was already moving toward the rifle cradled in the antlers above the fireplace. He had no idea if the old weapon was loaded. That question didn't really matter. It was the only option he had. If Grimm somehow lived through the encounter, Kincaid figured his own chances of a long life were nothing to brag about, but if Nabours and Skew killed the rancher, his odds would sink to the low end of the scale.

He swung, cocked, and fired the heavy Spencer in one continuous motion. The thumb-sized bullet caught Skew squarely in the breastbone, a fraction of a second too late. The skew-eyed cowboy still had time to pull the trigger of his Colt.

He was already falling when he did, though, and the slug, instead of speeding straight to Grimm's heart, slammed into the fleshy part of his buttock. The rancher braced himself against the wall with one hand and stared in disbelief at Skew, jerking spasmodically on the floor while a lake of blood pooled out beneath him.

To Nabours, the only object of interest in the room at that moment was the rifle in Kincaid's hand. He didn't think a one-armed man could lever another cartridge into the chamber quick enough, but he couldn't be sure. He wanted to pull his own six-gun and blow that damned hardheaded drifter into eternity, almost as much as he wanted to see the life spill out of Old Man Grimm like it was spilling out of Skew.

But he didn't have the nerve. He spun and crashed out through the door.

"Stop the sonofabitch!" Grimm shouted to no one in particular. Then he slid unconscious to the floor.

3

Kincaid had his own reasons—a thousand of them—for wanting to stop Nabours, but that cowboy flew out of the house as though the devil were a step behind, and gaining. His horse was standing ground-tied at the hitch rail. He vaulted into the saddle and gouged the gelding deep in the side with the spiked rowels of a Spanish spur. The startled pony took off in a burst of speed that almost cost Luke his seat in the saddle. But by the time Blondy had checked the loads in the rifle and made it to the door, Nabours was leaning low and riding hell-bent down a creek bed away from the ranch house.

For only a moment, Kincaid considered catching up his own horse and pursuing Luke Nabours. His mind was changed by the sickening throb in his head and shoulder and the sure knowledge he wouldn't get a hundred yards down the trail before he faded from the saddle. He turned and went back inside.

Dru Lee was kneeling beside her father, unfastening the massive silver belt buckle with its coiled-snake engraving and drawing his trousers down below his knees. Grimm's senses had returned, and with them his usual sulfuric humor.

"Dammit, girl, ain't you got no decency? Takin' down a man's pants while there's others about?"

He pulled weakly against her hand, then lay back. A moan echoed in the shadow of every breath he drew.

Blondy leaned the rifle against the stone fireplace, gathered up the rags and medicinal supplies from the table, and stepped across the room to place them beside the girl. The glance she gave him held no gratitude for the fact her father was still alive.

"You could be leaving right now," she said. "There's no one to stop you."

Kincaid studied her face for a moment, trying to read her thoughts.

"Thanks anyway," he said. "But I think I'll stick around just to see what fool thing breaks loose next. Your old man sure has a way about him when it comes to canning a hired hand."

Fire showed in her eyes.

"It wasn't his fault. You ought to know that. If you hadn't ridden onto Rafter G land and caught one of Dad's cows, this never would have happened."

Kincaid's tone was knife-edged.

"Don't believe everything those two yahoos told your dad. Seems to me you're having trouble deciding whose side you're on."

She was pouring turpentine into the gaping wound in the flesh of Grimm's hip. She opened her mouth to give him back an answer, but her words were drowned in a torrent of cursing.

"Dagnabit, girl!" the old rancher bellowed. "You tryin' to kill me? That's worse than the infernal bullet."

Instead of replying, she patted him gently on the shoulder, the loving gesture of a mother for an injured child. Then she looked up at Kincaid, the flame gone from her hazel eyes. He moved to the side of the wounded man, and between them they managed to wrest his solid bulk to the worn divan near the fireplace. There they laid him facedown and the girl set about completing her ministrations to the delicately situated wound.

From time to time, Dru Lee's eyes would stray to the body of Skew, sprawled in limp disarray against the far wall. Tears welled in her eyes and spilled down her cheeks. Blondy couldn't tell if it was concern over her father's wound or the ending of a man's life that provoked her grief.

A brightly colored hand-woven Indian rug lay spread on the floor just inside the door. Blondy caught up its edge, aligned it with the body of the dead man, and rolled the corpse inside it, a long, neat cylinder with blood soaking through here and there along its length. He heard Dru Lee's sharp intake of breath when Skew's head rolled back, his sightless eyes still open. Moving with care to protect the wound in his own shoulder, he dragged the body to the door and on out to the open porch.

Flies moved in quickly to sample the new find.

Back inside, Blondy collapsed into a chair, the throbbing in his head and shoulder intensified.

After a time he said, "You do have some more punchers on the place?"

"Of course." The words sounded unnatural, defensive. "Shorty, the foreman. And a Mexican. And . . ." She stopped. "They're out building branding pens."

Once begun, she seemed unable to stop talking.

"Dad hired Luke Nabours and the other one a couple of weeks ago. He had to have help with the roundup. I don't know what we'll do now."

"Hire some more hands," Blondy said.

"It's not that simple," she retorted, biting the words off sharply. "There aren't that many men looking for work."

Kincaid grinned without humor.

"Not for work on the Rafter G, anyway. After watching the gentle way your dad handled Luke, it's no wonder he has trouble hiring punchers."

Orlando Grimm had been lying quietly with his eyes closed, the corners of his mouth pinched down tightly. Now he opened his eyes and glared at Kincaid.

"You keep a civil tongue in your head, boy," he snapped. "How I treat hired hands is my business. I won't have no shiftless saddle tramp tryin' to tell me otherwise."

He pointed toward the archway to the kitchen.

"Get me that bottle of whiskey just inside the cupboard, boy."

"I'll get it, Dad," said the girl.

"No you won't. I won't have no daughter of mine soilin' her hands on such as that. He'll get it."

Blondy returned with the quart bottle of whiskey and handed it to Grimm.

"Better enjoy it. You've just used up all the orders you're ever going to give me, old man."

A gleam sprang to the deep-set eyes, a gleam that suddenly had Kincaid feeling uneasy.

"The hell you say." Grimm tilted the bottle and drank deeply, then set it carefully on the floor beside the divan. "Or don't you remember?"

"I remember shooting that off-eyed cowboy and saving your skin," Kincaid said. "Now I'm beginning to wonder why I bothered."

Grimm turned on his side, swore heatedly at the pain in his backside, but then stabbed a broad, hairy-backed finger at Blondy.

"You saved my life, I saved yours by not lettin' them two sidewinders string you up. That score is even."

A grin began to spread across Orlando Grimm's unlovely countenance. Blondy suddenly had the prickly feeling that he was riding into an ambush.

"I've got your word for a hundred and twenty dollars, young feller. When a man makes a promise like that, he don't back up from it. You savvy?"

Kincaid gritted his teeth against the effort to keep from swearing in the girl's presence.

"Why, you ornery old skinflint! You know your own man has hightailed it out of here with every cent of that money. If you hadn't gone off half-cocked and forced his hand, I'd have that money and you'd have your hundred and twenty. And maybe a couple of hired hands to help with your roundup."

Grimm's eyes closed to dark slits.

"All them ifs ain't worth a tinker's damn, boy. But I'm holding you to that promise. A hundred and twenty dollars. If you don't have it, I say that's tough. You can just work it off right here on the Rafter G!"

Blondy sucked in a breath, ready to tell the old man to go to hell, if they'd put up with him there. But a thought stopped him even while he was opening his mouth to speak. His bargain with Colonel Buchanan had brought him to the territory to find Orlando Grimm. He'd found him, all right, and now he had good reason to stay on at the Rafter G, study the situation, and then set about carrying out the Colonel's bidding.

Only thing was, nobody had told him he was going to be dealing with a lunatic.

At last he said, "Okay, Grimm. I'll stay

through roundup. At fifty a month."

The effect on the rancher was spectacular.

"Fifty a month? Why, you connivin' sneak thief! I've got a foreman that's been with me for nigh on twenty years, and he don't draw them kind of wages. I'll pay you half that."

"No deal," said Kincaid, getting to his feet. "Fifty a month or I walk out that door and you don't get a *centavo. Comprende?*"

A deep, wrenching groan rose from the old man's throat, and Blondy knew it wasn't from the pain of the wound in his nether regions. Money meant more to Orlando Grimm than a pint or two of blood. Even his own.

"All right," he breathed. "Fifty it is. But you'll by damn earn every penny of it."

Kincaid strode back to the divan and stood looking down at the Rafter G owner.

"Another thing while we're talking conditions. Don't ever raise your voice or your hand to me, mister. You do and you'll think lightning has struck. It's time you learned some manners."

Dru Lee had sat in silence at the foot of the divan while the two men talked. It was she who answered, and there was her father's stubborn defiance in her tone.

"You wouldn't dare talk to my father like that if he wasn't hurt. He's saved your life and given you a job. What more do you want?"

Her anger caused the freckles on her small nose to stand out sharply. Blondy found himself enjoying it. When he replied, he knew he was not being fair. She was, after all, within a year or two of his own age.

"I don't think your pa needs a wet-eared kid to fight his battles for him. Now, why don't you hush up and run along into the kitchen."

He only thought she'd been angry before. Now, like a blazing mesquite root showering sparks, her hazel eyes crackled with fire.

"You . . . you cow thief! I'm sorry I fed you and tied up your arm. Hanging's too good for the likes of you." She drew a quivering breath. "Dad, you don't want this . . . this gunfighter working for the Rafter G."

Blondy thought for a moment it was a smile he saw deep in Orlando Grimm's eyes, but then, that wasn't likely. He wasn't the smiling type.

"We'll make him earn every cent he draws, Dru Lee. Don't you worry none about him. I'll see he stays in his place."

He tried to sit up on the divan, but his face twisted in pain at the effort. He lay back against a pillow, muttered a curse under his breath, and glared blackly at Kincaid.

"Unless you're too crippled up to set a horse, go find Shorty and tell him you're workin' for me. You'll find him a coupla miles north of here tryin' to get them brandin' pens back in shape. Shorty's my ramrod, and a damn good man he is." He scowled. "Maybe you can do at least as much work as the Mex he's got helpin' him."

Blondy didn't reply. He found his bullet-punctured hat, placed it gingerly on the bandage about his head, and went out the door. The pain in his wounded shoulder throbbed with every step, but he set his jaw and forced it out of his mind. Old Man Grimm wasn't going to see him flinch. Nor was Grimm's high-tempered daughter.

4

The palomino was standing at the corral gate, still saddled and bridled. But the first horse Blondy went to was the rawboned buckskin that Skew had ridden. Sure enough, jammed into a worn saddlebag was his own six-gun and holster. Awkwardly, with one hand, he strapped the gunbelt about his waist. The familiar weight of it made him grunt with satisfaction.

He swung into the saddle and sent the stallion past the weathered outbuildings toward the beginnings of a ridge that angled northward. His cowman's eye told him the country was long overdue for moisture. The ridge he was following was a rocky hogback, here and there showing a patch of sagebrush but little else that would be of interest to a hungry cow. The buffalo grass in the swales on either side was sparse, already beginning to curl under the warm sun.

Ahead, the ridge ascended in a long slope, collecting patches of scrub cedar and piñon trees as it grew. In the distance, the high, ragged peaks of the San Cristobals still bore aprons of white. It was those snowcapped peaks that fed the cold quick waters of the Piedra River, the river which had almost been the grave of Blondy Kincaid. He shuddered at the recollection, then regretted the act. It had triggered a fresh stab of fire through his shoulder.

He heard swearing before he came in sight of the pens. Dropping off the crest of the ridge, he looked down into the bottom of a draw where two men were at work repairing a large pole corral, one of a network of pens for holding and branding cattle.

The cursing continued, carrying far in the clear mountain air. Kincaid appraised the scene and chuckled. At one end of a long, freshly peeled pole was a fat Mexican whose shirt was dark with perspiration. Holding the other end was a short, bowlegged cowboy with a ragged tobacco-stained beard. It was he who was doing the swearing, at the same time wringing his free hand.

"You pea-brained lump of ignorance. I don't know why yore ma didn't drown you in the Rio Grande River when you was borned.

If you wasn't so all-fired lazy you'd open your eyes once in a while and watch what you're doin'. You damn nigh broke my finger shovin' this pole agin' that post."

The Mexican was grinning a sheepish grin.

"Sí, Señor Shorty." He nodded. "You tell me to poosh it. So I poosh it."

Shorty was preparing to fire another broadside of invective at the Mexican, when he looked up and saw the man on the palomino coming down the slope. It never did any good to cuss Chorizo. All he did was grin and nod his head. If that stranger knew what was good for him, he'd ride on over the next hill and keep on riding. Shorty felt something less than hospitable at the moment.

Kincaid reined up.

"You the foreman?"

"What the hell's it to ya?"

"I'm looking for work."

"No, you ain't," the whiskered puncher snapped. "A man with just one good arm ain't worth the tits on a boar hog when it comes to cowboyin'. Now, just rattle yore hocks on outta here. And the sooner you're off the Rafter G, the better."

He turned his back on Kincaid and spat a brown stream of tobacco into the dust. Chorizo was leaning against a post watching the exchange.

"Hey, you no-account *frijole*-eater. Git your rear to movin'," the foreman barked.

The Mexican continued to lean against the post. Shorty became aware that he was looking up at the horseman. He spun back around.

"Is yore hearing crippled up too? I said git off the Rafter G. We've got all the punchers we need."

Deliberately Blondy hooked one leg over the saddle horn and began to roll a cigarette, making it appear easy despite the one-handedness.

"The Rafter G must not have much of a herd, what with you and the Mexican there being the only cowhands on the place."

Shorty sucked in a great lungful of air, preparing to singe the hide on the slender smart aleck sitting astride the palomino. But something about the stranger's manner told him he'd probably taken enough liberty with the newcomer's good nature.

"I'm gonna do you a favor," said Shorty. "I'm gonna explain it so it'll be plenty simple. We've got a few thousand head of mama cows and calves, and a right smart tally of yearlin' steers. And there's me and the Mex and a couple or three other full-growed cowboys and the tough old codger that owns this spread to look after 'em. Yeah, there's plenty to keep us busy, but we can handle it—if we don't have to spend half a day jawin' with every skinny, crippled-up bum that comes along lookin' for a handout."

Shorty was pleased with his speech. He worked a ragged square of chewing tobacco from a hip pocket and gnawed a corner from it with teeth that were worn, stained, and meager in number.

The man on the palomino appeared to be digesting the foreman's words, smoking in silence for a time while his eyes followed a quartet of cows and calves trailing single file out of a patch of scrub cedars a hundred yards away.

"I hate to be the one to tell you, old-timer. But as of an hour ago, the Rafter G is a mite shorthanded."

Shorty's eyelids drew down until they were mere slits in his leathery countenance.

"The more you talk, the less I like you, cowboy. What's that supposed to mean?"

"It means that Skew's dead, Luke's lit a shuck for parts unknown, and Old Man Grimm is laying on his belly with a chunk of lead in his backside. He hired me on to take up the slack."

Shorty's mouth hung open. A rivulet of tobacco-browned saliva ran down his chin and dropped onto his shirt front. The Mexican's eyes grew big. He crossed himself and murmured something under his breath.

Shorty shot a glance toward a worn .38-40 Winchester saddle gun propped against the pole fence a dozen paces away. He knew it was too far. But he hadn't survived sixty-eight years of Indian fighting, trail herding and ramrodding fractious cowhands to be easily intimidated.

"Hombre, you best start explainin' them words." He aimed a blunt, knobby finger at Kincaid's chest like the barrel of a derringer. "When I rode out this morning, all them fellas was plenty healthy and looked like they planned to stay thataway. Now you come ridin' up spinnin' a yarn that's mighty hard to swallow. If it's true, the first thing I want to know is, what did you have to do with it?"

The foreman knew it was a dangerous question, one that could have sudden, and fatal, consequences. He took a step backward, against the fence. And within reach of an ax leaning against a post.

Blondy read the thought in the old cowboy's eyes and suppressed a grin. He was reminded of a banty rooster, ready to tangle with any adversary that happened along, regardless of how badly overmatched he might be.

"If you think you're ready to listen, I'll tell you," he said.

"Try me," Shorty snapped.

"I was riding along in the river canyon, minding my own business, when that hombre with the bad eye shot me out of the saddle. That's what started it."

The foreman snorted.

"I ain't never seen him miss what he drew down on."

"That's how I come by this," Kincaid said, hooking a thumb toward his sheet-swathed shoulder.

"So when you got back on your feet, you plugged him and then went lookin' for the head man of the Rafter G. Is that it?"

"Try buttonin' your lip for a minute, you old coot." Blondy had withstood the cantankerous old cowboy's ill temper to the limit of his patience. "When we got to the house, Old Man Grimm and the one they call Luke got to arguin'. Skew, or whatever his name was, pulled his six-gun on Grimm and shot him in the hip. Luke took off. That's when I got the job punchin' cows for the Rafter G."

He flipped his cigarette into the dirt at Shorty's feet.

"That satisfy you?"

"Hell, no, it don't," bawled the foreman. "Grimm shot in the behind? And Skew dead? You ain't answered nothin' yet." He sucked in a deep breath. "How'd it happen?"

"You're plumb full of questions, *viejo*," Blondy grunted. "Skew missed his target because I blew out his light. Now do you get the picture?"

Shorty kicked at a dried cow chip.

"I ain't believin' you altogether," he said. "But I never did cotton to Skew and Nabours. They were pi'sen, in my books. I told the old man so."

He looked around at the corpulent Mexican, who had listened with fitful comprehension to Blondy's narrative.

"If that ain't a hell of a note," the foreman spat. "A Mex that cain't do anything right except stuff his gut, and a snip of a cowboy with only one good arm. And here it is roundup. What can you do with one hand? Besides roll a cigarette."

"What needs doing?" Blondy asked, innocent-faced.

"Now, what do you suppose goes on at brandin' time? Somebody's gotta rope 'em and somebody's gotta throw 'em and burn 'em. If you've cowboy'd any atall, you know there ain't no place at roundup for a cripple."

He spat into the dust again, scorn in the act, and speared a finger toward the collection of cows and calves moving along the trail a short distance away.

"You tell me how a one-armed jasper can be of any use. Like dabbin' a rope on a calf, fer instance."

Blondy had seen which way the conversation was heading. While the old man was finishing his tirade, he was taking down the horsehair lariat that swung in coils beneath the swell of his saddle. Abruptly he spurred the stallion toward the cows and calves.

The calf saw him coming but the big yellow horse was on him in an instant. Kincaid dropped the reins across the horse's neck and spun a double half-hitch around the saddle horn with the end of the rope. The loop he shook out was a brush cowboy's loop, hardly larger than the brim of Chorizo's hand-woven hat, but it settled over the calf's head with unerring accuracy.

The palomino knew what it was all about. He skidded to a stop on his haunches, pivoted about, and effortlessly dragged the protesting calf toward the two men standing beside the half-finished fence. Blondy hadn't touched the reins, letting the stud do the work he had been trained to do.

Shorty was impressed, but he tried not to show it.

"If you're half as smart as that claybank hoss is, we may get some work done after all."

The Mexican let his hand slide along the neck of the stallion.

"Que cavallo!" He grinned.

Shorty dragged the back of his hand across his mouth and pointed toward a timbered draw beyond the ridge.

"Me and the Mex have already cut and peeled enough poles to reach from here to the gulf. Make yourself and that rope useful and drag 'em in."

The sun was staining the western horizon the color of fresh blood when Blondy dragged in the last piece of timber. Shorty and Chorizo were sitting with their backs against the rail, the foreman in the act of fashioning a cigarette.

Kincaid stepped down from the saddle, very much aware of the aching stiffness in his shoulder. He sank to the ground beside a post and drew a deep, tired breath. Shorty was studying the cylinder of tobacco in his hand, and he didn't look up when he spoke.

"Judgin' from the rig on that hoss of yours, I'd say he's been workin' cattle in the Texas brush country. What would possess a man to leave that behind and come to these here mountains, I wonder?"

It was an oblique query, spoken in a casual manner that left plenty of room for Kincaid to answer or ignore it. Shorty was well aware that a man didn't pry into another man's business, where he was headed or why he'd departed where he'd been. But curiosity was prodding at him, and at his age he could afford to overlook some of the conventions of the range.

Kincaid spent an unnecessary half-minute layering dust on his cigarette butt with the sole of his boot. He had plenty of reason for coming to the New Mexico Territory, but it sure wasn't a reason he could talk about. Particularly to the foreman of the Rafter G. He muttered an oath to himself. A man with half a brain would've had his story worked out all neat and tidy long before now.

He squinted toward the leathery-faced old cowboy.

"Looking for somebody," he grunted.

Shorty's tone was casual.

"Lookin' to let a little daylight into 'em, I reckon."

"Nope. It's not a man I'm after."

The two heads, Shorty's and Chorizo's, swiveled about simultaneously.

"If that somebody ain't a man, then I reckon you really are courtin' trouble, pardner." The foreman grinned. "Must be a right special female."

"You hit it pretty close, old-timer." Blondy nodded. "Courtin' is what I had in mind. It's been quite a spell since I saw her, but the itch got so bad I had to scratch it. Rode all the way from Fort Worth to see if I could find her."

The whiskered old puncher snorted.

"Well, it ain't none of my business what a man wants to waste his time on." His gaze came to rest on the three horses cropping at the sparse grass. "I ain't never seen the woman yet I'd swap a good saddle horse fer. 'Ceptin' maybe that little Dru Lee gal."

Blondy closed one eye and squinted at Shorty through the other. He was remembering the fire in her hazel eyes.

"That ornery young'un? She's got the disposition of a black widow spider. I say she's been spoiled rotten by an old fool who thinks she can't do anything wrong. A good thrashing with a razor strap is what that little gal needs."

If he'd reached out and backhanded the little ranch foreman, the effect couldn't have been more pronounced. Shorty's head came around instantly. His faded blue eyes were stone-gray. Blondy began to wish he'd been a bit more tactful in his assessment of Dru Lee Grimm's character.

"You keep yore tongue to yourself about that little lady, cowboy. Else you're gonna find somethin' besides your arm in a sling. Nobody says such about Dru Lee without answerin' to me."

Shorty was on his feet, backed up against the pole fence. Blondy stood quickly, ready to block a fist if that's what the crusty ramrod had in mind.

"You act like a settin' hen with one chicken," he said to Shorty. "It's a hell of a note when a man can't speak his mind. It's no damned wonder the Rafter G can't get decent hands. No cowboy in his right mind would put up with a cantankerous bunch of mossbacks like this outfit breeds."

Shorty had his mouth open to reply, but something caused him to change his mind. He turned on a run-down boot heel, caught up the reins of his horse, and spurred away in a cloud of angry dust toward the headquarters of the Rafter G.

5

When Kincaid and Chorizo arrived, they found Shorty on a knoll a hundred yards from the house, hacking at the dry, brittle soil with a grubbing hoe. Down the slope a distance lay a long, irregular object wrapped in a colorful Indian rug.

Blondy pulled the palomino to a halt and sat the saddle watching the foreman laboring at the grave. It wasn't the first time the knoll had been used for such a purpose. There were other mounds of hard-packed earth in a line beyond the point where Shorty was doing his digging.

The wizened, bewhiskered puncher ignored the two riders and continued digging for a time. Finally he stopped, slid his ancient hat from his head, and wiped the perspiration from his brow with the sleeve of his shirt. His gaze was on Chorizo, who was nervously and unsuccessfully trying to ignore the blanket-encased corpse of Skew.

"Get down off that hoss and make yourself useful, you shiftless *frijole*-eater," he said. "You've got a choice. Either dig this hole or drag that stiff up the hill."

Chorizo rolled his eyes heavenward and climbed with ungainly grace from his saddle. He sent another glance toward the cadaver and reached out to take the heavy hoe from Shorty's hands.

"First dadblamed time I've ever known him to volunteer for hard work," he muttered to no one in particular. But Blondy saw it was the old man's way of offering a truce. He said nothing.

The planting of Skew took another half-hour and used up the last of the daylight. After the horses were unsaddled and fed, the three headed for the ranch house. The yellow gleam of a coal-oil lamp was sifting through the windows.

Dru Lee was placing the meal on the table. Blondy had decided he wasn't interested in what she was doing or how she looked while doing it. But his eyes, of their own volition, followed her movements from the kitchen stove to the table. She had done something to her hair and was wearing a shirt she had outgrown. It made her waist look tiny and the rest of her more woman than girl.

Then he saw that she had set six places. And there were only five of them. Unless she'd forgotten that Skew was dead and Nabours had taken off like a turpentined cat. But there was no mention of it as they took their seats.

Blondy had the first bit of steak halfway to his mouth when the door opened. He heard a sound from Dru Lee and saw her heart swell into her eyes. He turned his head and saw the man coming through the door and wondered at the instant dislike which formed in his mind.

Dru Lee moved quickly to take the newcomer's hat. He was in the act of sitting down at the sixth plate when he saw Kincaid.

"Who's this?" It was more than a question. It was a pronouncement that they all should prepare for his approval or disapproval.

His dark eyes swept round the table, and he asked the next question before the first could be answered.

"Where's the boss?"

Shorty waved his fork in the air.

"You've shore missed out on it, Garrett," he said. "Had us a mite of excitement around here today. Ended up with the boss taking a slug in his backside. It all happened after this here feller showed up in the river canyon."

The newcomer looked Blondy squarely in the eyes, but his question was directed to Shorty.

"I asked who he is."

"Name's Kincaid," the foreman replied hastily. "Rode onto the Rafter G this mornin' and got all crossways with Luke Nabours and Skew."

It was no longer curiosity that Kincaid saw in the big man's face. It was hostility. He didn't like what he was hearing.

"I'll talk to Grimm," he said.

"Garrett, he's asleep now," said Dru Lee almost plaintively. "He needs to rest."

But Garrett ignored her words and went on toward the back of the house. Silence lay across the dining table.

"I gather he belongs here," Blondy said at last.

"That's right." Dru Lee's answer was sharp, emphatic. "He belongs here."

Shorty washed down a mouthful of food with a swallow of coffee and looked at Kincaid.

"Garrett Haley's his name. He's a pretty fair hand when it comes to punchin' cows." He turned and looked at Dru Lee. "He ain't gonna be happy when he finds out Luke and

Skew ain't around no more."

The foreman's prediction was correct. Haley strode back into the room with a black scowl across his face. He jerked his chair out and sat down. Dru Lee was up instantly to pour his coffee.

"It's a hell of a note," Haley said, glaring at Kincaid. "Losing two good men right here at roundup. And getting a crippled-up shirttail drifter in return." His next words to Blondy were a challenge. "Do you know anything about workin' cattle?"

Blondy let the question hang in the air for a long moment. Then he said, "Maybe. You need a lesson?"

Haley's darkly handsome face began to grow crimson. His mustache stood out from his lip like the hackles along an angry dog's neck. Shorty felt the heat of the tension.

"He's pretty handy with a rope, Garrett," the foreman said hurriedly. "Even with that bum arm. We'll get it done, all right."

The tone of Shorty's words and the deference in Dru Lee's behavior plagued Kincaid's thoughts throughout the meal. Afterward he and Shorty and Chorizo headed for the bunkhouse, while Haley remained behind talking to the girl.

Hunkered down against the front of the little building, Blondy fashioned a cigarette and offered the makings to Shorty.

"This Haley hombre," Blondy said offhandedly. "What's his game? He acts like he's the ramrod of this outfit."

"Hell no, he ain't the ramrod," Shorty snapped. "I give the orders around this lash-up. And don't you forget it!"

But there was something about the words that fell just short of conviction. Blondy couldn't resist prodding the cranky little foreman.

"Wasn't that you bragging on him a little bit ago?"

Shorty shot his cigarette butt away in a shower of sparks.

"I said he was a good hand. I didn't say anything about likin' him."

It was more than an idle urge to heckle Shorty that drove Blondy to ask the next question.

"Appears to me as though he rates pretty high in Dru Lee's eyes. Care to tell me about it?"

It was so long before Shorty answered that Kincaid thought he was simply going to ignore the question. When the foreman finally replied, the words seemed almost to cause him physical pain.

"This is just between you and me and the gatepost, savvy? Haley came along a couple of years ago, when we was needin' a hand real bad. Pitched in and did a fine job, but then he stayed on through the winter without nobody askin' him to."

He spat into the dust at Blondy's feet.

"Old Man Grimm ain't all that taken with him either, I reckon."

Blondy grunted in disgust.

"If you ask me, neither of you old mossbacks is very bright. Letting a second-rate cowboy stay on the payroll just to keep a half-grown kid happy."

Shorty got to his feet.

"Nobody asked you," he growled.

They went inside the bunkhouse, where Chorizo was already fast asleep and snoring raucously. Blondy surveyed the smoke-blackened walls and the random .44-caliber holes where someone had taken a shot at a mouse or a fly, and decided it was a duplicate of all the other bunkhouses in which he'd slept. He hoped that didn't mean it had to be populated with bedbugs.

He awoke in the predawn darkness to a gut-deep pain in his wounded shoulder. Shorty offered to pack it with the cud of tobacco in his mouth, but Blondy chose instead to soak the bandage again with coal oil. During the previous evening's meal, Dru Lee made no mention of redressing the wound. All she could think of was Garrett what's-his-name, Blondy thought wryly.

Dru Lee had breakfast on the table as the eastern horizon grew pink with the new day. Blondy surveyed the meal of steak and biscuits and eggs and coffee and marveled. Old Man Grimm might be as tight as the knot in a wet lariat when it came to paying wages, but he sure didn't skimp on the groceries.

To his surprise, Orlando Grimm was at the table, ready to eat. He was sitting aslant in a big chair, a pillow beneath the hip where Skew's bullet had entered. Pain still etched deep lines in his face, but there was none of the resignation Kincaid had seen there the previous day. Grimm was once again in charge. Garrett Haley was nowhere in sight.

"How'er those pens comin'?" Grimm demanded of Shorty.

The foreman wasn't intimidated by Grimm's tone.

"They're finished and ready to go. But I'll tell you one thing. It ain't going to be easy gathering and branding every critter on the place, with no more help than I've got. We need some more hands."

Grimm's brow was puckered in a deep scowl.

"Hell, I know that. But there ain't a puncher anywhere along the Piedra that'll hire on with the Rafter G, thanks to Slick Detwiler, the damned polecat. He's pi'sened everybody in the whole territory agin' me. You boys are going to have to handle it yourselves."

Shorty didn't bother to look up, but went on eating.

"Huh!" he grunted. "Won't be the first time we've worked shorthanded at roundup."

Innocently Blondy asked the question: "Where's Haley?"

Silence heavy enough to carve with a butcher knife lay over the table. Neither Grimm nor Shorty looked up. It was Dru Lee who answered, her tone defensive.

"He's still asleep."

"Must be nice," Kincaid said, half to himself. But she heard it.

"He does more work around here than anyone!" Her face was growing crimson. "He's been riding at night. That's why he sleeps in the house instead of the bunkhouse. So he can get some rest. If everybody else worked just half as hard as he does—"

Blondy interrupted, looking at Grimm.

"Riding at night? Don't believe I've ever

heard of an outfit carrying on a roundup in the dark. Seems sort of strange."

Both Grimm and Shorty were suddenly preoccupied with what was on their plates. To Kincaid's surprise, it was Dru Lee who broke the silence again, but the anger was gone from her voice.

"You see, Dad. I told you it didn't seem right."

Grimm looked at his daughter, solicitude on his countenance.

"Now, girl, he's just keepin' his eyes on some things. Don't you worry none about it." He swung his head about until he was glaring at Blondy. "You! You mind your own business and let me do the runnin' of the Rafter G. Hear?"

They were heading for the corral to catch up their mounts when Blondy said, "Tell me about this Slick Detwiler gent. What's the beef between him and Old Man Grimm?"

Shorty's eyebrows moved up a couple of wrinkles.

"If I didn't know before that you was a stranger to these parts, I'd sure know it now. Everybody knows that Slick Detwiler is the biggest cowman in these parts. His Hatchet outfit takes in just about everything on this side of the Piedra, but he ain't happy with that. He wants it all. He's tried for years to crowd the Rafter G out, but Old Man Grimm can sure match him for stubborn."

Blondy's gaze wandered away toward the distant San Cristobal Mountains, showing black against the indigo of the early-dawn sky.

"That Dru Lee. She sort of takes after her old man," he said.

Shorty saw nothing extraordinary in the comment.

"As fine a little gal as they come. You can hang your hat on that."

"What became of Mrs. Grimm?"

Shorty's first impulse was to tell the tall, blond cowboy to keep his nose out of other folks' affairs. Blondy could see it on his face. But abruptly his expression softened.

"Died when Dru Lee was born, I guess. That little gal never knew her mama." He paused, and when he spoke again he was looking away, so that Kincaid couldn't see his face. "Nobody could have done a finer job of lookin' after a young'un than Grimm has."

They were at the corral, and as the foreman started in to catch his horse, Blondy stopped him.

"That palomino of mine needs a rest."

Shorty nodded.

"Yeah, it looks like you'll be around for a spell. You can ride that stocking-legged sorrel yonder, and swap off with the big bay."

Kincaid procured his horsehair rope and dropped a loop over the sorrel's head. The instant he felt the rope settle, the gelding quieted and stood docilely while Blondy, swearing at his one-handed awkwardness, drew the saddle down.

Shorty and Chorizo were mounted and waiting when Blondy led the sorrel outside the gate and stepped into the saddle. He realized too late he should have mounted while he was still inside the fence. Before he could gather up the reins, the sorrel ducked his head and broke into a wild, bone-jarring fit of bucking.

The pain in his shoulder was hell. Kincaid gritted his teeth and clamped his legs tight around the sorrel's barrel. He knew he was better off in the jerking, popping saddle than he would be hitting the ground.

After a time the gelding got it out of his system. Blondy drew the makings from his shirt pocket, trying to appear casual. Shorty had a pained expression on his face.

"Well, doggone my hide," he said. "I plumb forgot to mention it. That old pony always does that early in the morning. Never could seem to break him of the habit."

Kincaid eyed the foreman with grim humor as he ran his tongue along the cylinder of tobacco.

"If he does it again, I'll break him. I'll shoot the son-of-a-gun right square between the eyes."

They left the ranch house behind and rode north through the low, broken hills to the deep, ragged gorge that caged the plunging waters of the Piedra River. They drew rein and Shorty waved his hand in an arc toward the east.

"It's Rafter G all the way to where the Little Red runs into the Piedra. You probably crossed that comin' in." He turned and stabbed a hand westward, as though there was something distasteful in that direction. "We join Detwiler's spread over yonder."

He pushed his hat to the back of his head.

"See that queer-lookin' streak of gray just to the left of the Piedra? That's Lame Horse Bluffs. A natural boundary between the Rafter G and the Hatchet, as good as any fence you'll ever see. But I've still heard that Detwiler is thinkin' about stringin' bobbed wire around his outfit. Be just like the old bastard."

The very lip of the river canyon was suddenly before them. Far below, the angry, turbulent, snow-fed waters of the Piedra crashed in frothy madness along the boulder-shot riverbed, on their headlong plunge to join the Rio Grande. It was wild, brutal country.

"It's going to take us a right smart bit of time to shake every bush along this river, but that's what we're going to do," the foreman said, taking in the serpentine length of the gorge with a wave of his hand. "Some of them critters are wild as deer. But we're rounding up everything with hair on it."

Kincaid frowned.

"Cattle prices are still holding good. What's Grimm going to do next year if he sells off his entire herd?"

Shorty hooked a knee over his saddle horn.

"Grimm has his own ideas about where the cow business is heading. But you let him worry about that. You worry about gatherin' cattle."

He straightened in the saddle.

"We best quit jawin' and get to poppin' brush."

He jerked a thumb toward the east, where the sun was breaking away from the horizon.

"Chorizo, you work that direction, all the way to the Little Red. I'll take this stretch in the middle. And you ride from here west,

Kincaid. I'm givin' you a break today."

He turned and motioned behind them to the draw that fell away to the south in a broad, shallow triangle, its apex leading into the pens on which they had completed repairs the previous day.

"This is where we want 'em," he said, and started to rein his horse away. Abruptly he pulled up and turned about, and Blondy had the unmistakable impression that the ramrod's next statement wasn't nearly as casual a remark as he wanted it to appear.

"One more thing, Kincaid. You'll be ridin' toward Lame Horse Bluffs, up against Detwiler's range. Even though the bluffs are on Rafter G ground, I want you to stay plenty clear of them. Savvy?"

What he said needed more explanation, and Blondy opened his mouth to ask. But Shorty jerked his tough little gray horse around and spurred him away along the canyon's rim. Chorizo, astride a big-boned roan, had already loped away to the east, appearing graceful and easy in the saddle despite his bulk.

A fresh breeze in his face, Kincaid rode westward. Despite the stiffness in his shoulder and a tenderness in his scalp from the bullet wounds, he felt good. He was doing what he preferred to do: sit the saddle on a good cow pony in the middle of a world that stretched in every direction as far as the eye could see. Then, perversely, his contentment vanished. He'd all but forgotten what it was that had brought him to the heart of the New Mexico Territory in the first place: a bitter old man's obsession to destroy an enemy he hadn't set eyes on in twenty years. Colonel Webster Buchanan had managed to maneuver Kincaid into the kind of corner there wasn't any getting out of without paying too high a price.

He swore into the wind and pushed the thought from his mind.

The face of the land along the Piedra River was seamed and broken by endless small canyons that gave into the main gorge, and concealed in the shinnery and scrub cedars and dwarf piñon trees, Kincaid found his quarry. But as Shorty had predicted, it was like trying to gather so many wild deer. For every half-dozen cows and calves that he managed to chouse from the ravines, a dozen would slip past him and dive back into the underbrush.

In two hours' time the sorrel was blowing hard and lathered with sweat, and Kincaid could count his gather on both hands. But those he pushed out onto the bald ridges, toward the pens several miles distant.

Noon came and went without notice. Kincaid had spent enough of his life working cattle to know that most outfits couldn't afford the luxury of a noontime break for a meal. A man who couldn't get by from breakfast to supper with a cigarette and another notch out of his belt had best look for work in a bank or a dry-goods store.

The afternoon wore on, Blondy beginning to feel he'd already made a fair stab at earning Grimm's fifty-a-month largess. The sun was still a good hour from the mountain-ribbed horizon to the west when Kincaid came near to the wall of stone that Shorty had pointed out to him early in the day.

The old ramrod's words had fallen considerably short of doing justice to Lame Horse Bluffs.

It was a one-sided fortress of limestone, a wall that shot straight up into the air for three hundred feet or more. One end of the wall jutted out over the rim of the Piedra River, while the other, running away from the river gorge at a ninety-degree angle, was lost somewhere in the distant tree-cloaked hills. It was as though the Creator had considered cutting the world in two right about here but had changed his mind after hewing through several hundred feet of stone.

Blondy pulled up his horse a half-mile from the bluffs. He rolled a cigarette and let his gaze take in the gray-green sweep of vegetation that began at the base of the abrupt rocky ridge at his feet and rolled away to the base of the stone butte. It was a huge triangle, girded on two sides by the great limestone escarpment and the sharp ridge on which he now stood, and on the third side by the precipitous plunge into the Piedra River gorge. Within that three-sided cul de sac was a tightly woven forest of low-branched piñons, gnarled cedars, and red-tipped, spine-armored cholla cactus.

Grass was good across the little valley, better than on the hills and slopes behind him. If this strange trap had a natural water supply, it would be an almost perfect habitat for cattle, Blondy mused. A hundred head, or a thousand, could be concealed in the undergrowth.

He shook his head. It was passing strange that Shorty would warn him to stay clear of the bluffs, as likely a hideaway for Rafter G livestock as any covert he'd come across.

Kincaid was scrutinizing the underbrush for signs of cattle when his eye registered a movement along the spine of the great vertical bluff in the distance. He studied the jagged stone rim for a time before he spotted the movement again. For an instant he saw a lone horseman silhouetted against the late-afternoon sky. Then the rider disappeared into the trees.

Blondy shrugged, thankful that the motion no longer caused more than a dull ache in his wounded shoulder, and rode on along the crown of the ridge. Minutes later he saw a stirring in the fringe of the underbrush and gave chase to a longhorned brindle cow and her offspring. The horseman on the cliff was instantly forgotten.

The sorrel knew his work, but the cow and calf had the fierce instinct of wild animals. By the time Blondy had cut the pair off from the edge of the thicket and had them heading along the barren ridge, he had worked along the near side of the triangle until he was less than a quarter-mile from the limestone bluff.

He had the sorrel in a high lope, crowding the fugitives up the bald slope, when it happened. Abruptly, without warning, the gelding started falling forward. He plunged to his knees and crashed into the ground. Blondy threw himself from the saddle an instant before the horse flipped over onto his back.

It was while the ground was rushing up to

meet him that he heard the sound of the shot. He rolled away from the tumbling horse to the scant shelter of a rotted tree trunk. He lay there on his belly, scanning the skyline to the west and feeling the warmth of the blood trickling across his chest from the reopened wound in his shoulder.

The sorrel was fighting to get to his feet, but he succeeded only in thrashing about helplessly. After a time he quit straining and lay back, his nostrils quivering and his eyes rolling wildly.

The horse was Kincaid's first concern, but reason kept him concealed behind the rotted log. The distance from the rim of the bluff to his location was a long one, but not so long that he couldn't be picked off with a lucky shot from some long-distance cannon like a Sharps buffalo gun. And there was still plenty of daylight in which to do it.

Silence settled around him. The brindle cow and her calf had vanished back into the thicket as quickly as a pair of cottontail rabbits when the pursuit had been interrupted. Several paces away lay the sorrel.

As Blondy watched, the horse struggled once more to rise, the effort bringing a squall of fright and despair from his throat. To hell with the risk, Kincaid decided, and he began to crawl on hands and knees to the downed animal.

One glance was enough. The horse had been shot through both front legs. A buffalo gun, without question. One foreleg was hanging by a tendon, the bullet having shattered the cannon bone just below the knee. The other leg was also shot through. Blood oozed from the wound to soak the white stocking with a bright red stain.

Blondy sat on his heels for several minutes, cursing softly. Cantankerous the sorrel may have been when first saddled, but he'd worked his heart out all day.

Disregarding the distant bushwhacker, Kincaid got to his feet. With his left hand he drew the Colt from his hip and in one continuous motion cocked the hammer and fired. The bullet etched a black hole squarely in the middle of the tiny white star on the sorrel's forehead.

He was still standing there with his gun in his hand when he heard the horses beating toward him along the ridge. He looked up and saw Shorty and Chorizo bearing down on him.

The foreman, in the lead, pulled his horse to a stop on its haunches and shoved his hat to the back of his head.

"Hell's bells, Kincaid," he growled. "I didn't know you was serious about it when you threatened to break him of his bad habits permanent."

6

Hunkered down against the carcass of the dead horse, Kincaid rolled a cigarette and told the foreman and the Mexican cowboy what had happened. The raw edge of the great bluff, the lair of the bushwhacker, was now only a silhouette against the evening sky.

The last word was barely out of Blondy's mouth when Shorty broke in.

"Dammit to hell! I told you to stay clear of the bluffs, Kincaid. But, no! You've got to ignore orders and ride where you was told not to. And look what it got you."

With an effort, Blondy kept his voice calm.

"I thought you told me Grimm's outfit ran all the way to Lame Horse Bluffs. Don't that mean we're still on the Rafter G?"

Shorty waved his fist in the air.

"It means just what I said. When you're told to stay clear of the bluffs, you stay clear.

Savvy? Now, forget about it and gather up your riggin'."

"Forget about it! Not on your life. As soon as I can get another horse under me, I'm going looking for the sidewinder that did this."

"No, you ain't," Shorty snapped. "Now, get your gear and let's head for home."

Blondy's wrath was still smoldering as he pulled the bridle from the dead horse's head and unfastened the cinches of his saddle. What the hell kind of outfit was this? he swore as he jerked at the saddle, pinned to the ground by twelve hundred pounds of deadweight. Finally, reluctantly, he had to ask for help.

Chorizo dropped a loop on his lariat over the saddle horn and let his horse do the work. When the saddle was free, the Mexican pulled it up and lashed it to the fork of his own saddle.

"Come on," Shorty said to Kincaid. "Get up here behind me. It won't kill you."

They rode into the headquarters of the Rafter G that way, Blondy behind Shorty's saddle. It was humiliating. A cowboy who wasn't able to ride back to the corral with the horse he'd left on that morning was an object of scorn, regardless of the reason he'd been put afoot.

Orlando Grimm didn't make it any easier. He was sitting on the porch in the light of a lantern when the two horses and three men rode in. He waited until they had unsaddled and turned the horses out.

"Did these old eyes deceive me, or was that you stealin' a ride behind Shorty? I swear I don't know how a man can work cattle ridin' behind somebody else."

Kincaid was tempted to give the old rancher the benefit of his thoughts, but decided it was an issue he didn't care to call attention to. He went on to the bar of soap and basin of water standing at the back door.

Dru Lee was quiet and reserved as she went about serving the meal to the three latecomers. As before, there was the sixth place set at the table, but Garrett Haley was nowhere in sight.

Orlando Grimm was in a talkative mood. He wanted to know every detail of the day's work, and particularly the specifics of the misfortune that had befallen Kincaid.

In the barest collection of words, Blondy told him what had happened.

"Did you get a look at him?" Grimm asked.

"Nope. Too late and too far away. But I'll tell you what he looks like this time tomorrow, because I'm heading after him at first light."

Grimm's reaction was an echo of Shorty's.

"No you ain't. Not while you're drawin' Rafter G pay. No puncher of mine is going to wander off on a wild-goose chase smack in the middle of roundup."

Kincaid gritted his teeth.

"No one takes a shot at me without paying for it. I figure I can track him down in a day, two at the outside. Then I'll worry about your roundup."

To his surprise, Grimm didn't explode in a fit of expletives. Instead, his tone was imploring.

"I can savvy your wantin' to settle things with that bushwhacker, young feller. But time's growin' short. I need every hand on the place."

It was the money that did it, Blondy saw. If it had to do with money, Orlando Grimm could be reasonable. But there was one question the old man hadn't answered.

"Tell me this," Blondy said. "If you're so all-fired hard-up for riders, why don't you give that Haley hombre something to do? Or is he allergic to hard work?"

Dru Lee's head snapped around as though his words had been the lash of a whip.

"Just you keep your mouth shut about him! What he does is no concern of yours."

Grimm's tone was only mildly remonstrative.

"You've got an awful bad habit of pokin' your nose into places where it don't belong, Kincaid."

Blondy wasn't exactly sure why he felt an urge to pursue the subject, except that Dru Lee had such a hair-trigger temper when it came to a discussion of Garrett Haley. The sound of a footstep at the door behind him nudged him on. He kept his voice innocently casual.

"Well, it does seem a mite strange to let a perfectly healthy puncher lay up and sleep all day while there's work to be done. Doggone me if my conscience wouldn't hurt something fierce if I was to do that."

The footstep in the doorway had been that of Garrett Haley, and now the big man strode to the place on the opposite side of the table and jerked the chair back with his broad hands. His face was hard, his mouth a straight line, white at the corners.

"Just who the hell you talking about?" he demanded in a strained tone.

A smile pulled at Kincaid's lips.

"Why, anybody that fits the description, I suppose."

Haley glared at him for a long moment.

"One of these days I'm gonna teach you some manners," he said through clenched teeth. "Just as soon as you've got two good arms."

"Don't do me any favors," Blondy said easily.

Dru Lee began hurriedly to fill Haley's plate. Kincaid took a perverse pleasure in seeing the nervousness his caustic remark had produced.

As was his insensitive way, Orlando Grimm chose that moment to open another subject with Haley. But his tone lacked the iron that Blondy had come to expect.

"We're runnin' mighty shorthanded on roundup, Garrett. Need you to ride with Shorty and the other boys, startin' tomorrow."

Haley stopped eating and looked at Grimm steadily. Kincaid thought for a brief instant it was contempt he saw mirrored in Haley's eyes.

"The hell, you say," the black-mustached cowboy grunted. "I'll tell you when I'm finished with what I'm doin', old man."

Kincaid read the expressions around the table in amazement. Shorty's features reflected repressed rage. Grimm's face was wooden. He dropped his eyes to his plate and worried pointlessly with his fork at a piece of meat. Dru Lee said, "Now, Garrett," under her breath.

Kincaid looked into her eyes and saw a battle raging there. Her affection, or whatever it was she felt for Garrett Haley, wasn't enough to excuse his disrespect to her father. She looked up at that moment and her gaze met Blondy's. She looked quickly away, but not before her cheeks had flushed a flaming crimson.

For an instant her self-assurance was stripped away, and for that instant Blondy felt a surge of pity for her and her lifetime of indenture in a household of men. Garrett Haley was probably the first eligible man she had ever had an opportunity to know.

Shorty broke the prolonged silence.

"Tolerable late," he muttered, then got to his feet and moved self-consciously toward the door. Chorizo followed. Kincaid was tempted to pursue the subject of Haley's strange place in the Rafter G's work scheme, but another glance at Dru Lee's still-flaming face changed his mind. He got up and followed the other two cowboys toward the bunkhouse.

On his bunk in the darkness of the shack, Blondy smoked a cigarette and listened to Shorty getting settled. After a time he said, "I'll stick it out through roundup. But I'll get that coyote that shot my horse out from under me. I'm not about to forget it."

Shorty made no reply.

The next morning, though, his resolve to track down the bushwhacker faded into the background. He and Shorty and Chorizo rode away from the ranch house before dawn and topped the ridge above the branding pens at first light, and pulled up there to smoke a cigarette and give the new day a chance to come to life.

"Something fishy," said Kincaid. "It's awful quiet. Too quiet. Looks like those cows and calves we brought in yesterday would be bawlin' their fool heads off."

But there were no sounds from the pens below. As the first rays of daylight washed into the swale, the three pairs of eyes strove to see through the gloom. In minutes they had their answer.

"I'll be a sonofabitch!" Shorty breathed.

"*No creo!*" muttered the Mexican.

Blondy was the first to regain his senses. He spurred the palomino stud down the slope and reined up where he had sat the first day and watched the foreman and the Mexican sweating in the sun while they labored to construct the pens.

Now those pens were in shambles. The wreckage resembled a giant handful of oversized wheat straw tossed about by a whirlwind.

"Somebody just roped the posts and broke them off," Kincaid said. "Then he tied onto the poles and drug 'em away. And turned every one of those cows and calves back into the breaks."

He swore into the breaking day.

"I'd take a guess and say it was probably Luke Nabours."

But Shorty was off his horse, down on one knee inspecting the powdered earth.

"Nope," he said after a moment. "One man couldn't have done this much damage. And there's the tracks of three or four different hosses. It took a pretty good crew to do this job."

They were halfway back to the house, each man preoccupied with his own thoughts, before Kincaid broke the silence.

"If I was a man with a suspicious nature, I'd begin to suspect somebody has it in for the Rafter G. First they take a shot at me and get my horse. Then they wreck the pens and turn loose every critter we've gathered."

He looked at Shorty.

"Who do you figure did it? And why in blue blazes would they?"

The Rafter G ramrod was looking straight ahead. His gaze didn't waver from that point.

"Beats hell out of me."

It was all he said. Finally Blondy turned to Chorizo.

"How about it? Any ideas?"

The Mexican drew his huge shoulders up and let them drop. He didn't look at Blondy either.

Orlando Grimm was again sitting on the porch, absorbing the rays of the freshly risen sun. One hip was propped on a pillow.

"What in the name of good sense are you hombres doin' here?" he demanded. "There's livestock to be gathered, and daylight's a-wastin'."

Shorty spat a stream of tobacco juice into a morning-glory vine beside the porch step. In terse sentences punctuated with curses, he told the rancher what they had found.

As the brief narrative reached its conclusion, Grimm's face grew livid. He sprang to his feet, then grabbed the wounded hip and sat back down. Halfway through a string of curses, he stopped. Blondy saw the great effort with which he returned to a semblance of calm, and he began to perceive the strength that lay at the foundation of Orlando Grimm's sulfurous nature.

A knobby length of cholla trunk was in his hands, for use as a walking cane. Now his broad hands gripped it until his knuckles turned white. But his voice was relatively calm.

"Boys, what's done is done. There ain't no use cryin' over spilt milk. There's only one thing to do. Rebuild them pens and start gatherin' them critters again."

Kincaid twisted about in his saddle and looked at Shorty. Now surely the ramrod would be ready to fight! But the aging foreman sat without expression, one knee hooked around his saddle horn.

Blondy turned back to the man on the porch.

"Has everybody in this outfit gone loco? They shoot a horse and wreck a string of pens and undo half the work of a roundup. Next thing, they'll be stealing you blind, running off every head of stock on the place. And you just roll over and play dead."

The silence that followed drew out for a full half-minute, except for some clearing of throats. When Grimm spoke, the words were hard, but their usual cutting edge was missing.

"As long as I'm runnin' the Rafter G, you'll do like I tell you, Kincaid. Don't forget that."

He shifted on the pillow to ease his wounded hip.

"You won't be much use buildin' fence with that crippled-up arm. I want you to ride into Arrowhead and hire us another hand. I don't care if you have to hold a gun to his head, just get him out here. Shorty, you and the Mex will have to start all over. Puttin' it off won't make it any easier."

Kincaid was turning away when Grimm stopped him.

"Hitch up that little bay mare to the buckboard. I'm sending Dru Lee in to get some things. You ride along and keep an eye on her."

Dru Lee came out of the house five minutes later. Blondy stood beside the wheel of the buckboard and offered his arm to help her up. She ignored him, and drove away while he was getting to his horse.

The road that led away from the Rafter G headquarters was hardly more than a faint pair of tracks. There wasn't a great deal of travel between this ranch and anywhere else in the world, Kincaid concluded.

He caught up with the wagon and spurred the stallion on ahead, moving through rolling hills dotted with piñon trees, sagebrush, and an occasional yucca. In the distance, across an undulating ocean of ridges and canyons, the terrain grew ragged and then melted into stairstep terraces of purples and shades of indigo. At the very rim of the globe, the softly molded mountains dissolved into the azure of the morning sky until a man's eye could no longer be certain where the earth left off and the heavens began.

They rode in silence for an hour until Blondy slowed his horse and let the buckboard draw alongside. The more he thought about it, the sillier it seemed not to have some conversation to season the journey. And besides, he wanted another look into the depths of those hazel eyes.

He pushed his hat back as the palomino fell in beside the front wheels of the wagon.

"I never did thank you properly for patching up my shoulder, ma'am."

She glanced up at him from beneath the brim of her low-crowned, broad-brimmed hat. There was suspicion in her gaze, as though she was prepared for his comment to be a sarcastic one.

"That's not necessary," she said carefully. "I'd do the same for anyone."

There was no invitation in her tone, but Blondy went on as though she had smiled warmly.

"Yessir, you're about as good as any sawbones that's ever fished a chunk of lead out of this carcass."

In spite of herself, it seemed, she responded.

"You've been shot before?"

"Well, yes. A few times. Nothing fatal, though."

When she spoke again, she didn't meet his eyes but kept her gaze forward, over the ears of the bay mare.

"Why did you come to this part of the country?"

"No particular reason," Kincaid said, watching her face carefully. "Just drifting."

She looked up quickly at him.

"Shorty said you were looking for someone. A girl."

A scowl darkened Blondy's face. He would have to remember to keep his stories straight.

"Shorty talks too much," he said.

"Is it true?"

He avoided her eyes.

"Yeah, I suppose so."

"What's she like?" The question was more than polite conversation. It made Blondy uneasy.

"Well, you know. A girl. It's been a long time since I've seen her."

"Does she live near here?"

Kincaid didn't enjoy the direction the talk had taken, but more than that, he didn't like lying to this straightforward, sort of cute girl. It would have made his life a great deal simpler if Orlando Grimm hadn't had a daughter.

"I don't know," he said. "I don't know where she is."

His reply was sharper than he had intended. He regretted it.

"Tell me something," he went on. "Who is it that's fighting the Rafter G? Who do you think tore down the pens and took a shot at me?"

She shook her head.

"There's only one man it can be. Slick Detwiler. And his Hatchet outfit."

He grunted in acknowledgment.

"Your pa seems to attract trouble like a lightning rod. What's everybody got against the Rafter G, anyway?"

She was instantly defensive.

"It's not Dad's fault. You don't know how

he's had to scrap for what we have. Ever since he came to this country—even before I was born—he's had to fight the big ranchers. Slick Detwiler isn't the first. There was one, a long time ago, who tried everything he could to run Dad out of the territory. But Dad doesn't give up easily."

Kincaid nodded.

"I can see that. But it still doesn't make sense. Detwiler, for instance. Why would he risk a range war to get his hands on the Rafter G? Your pa's range isn't anything to brag about, what with it being so dry. And I don't suppose it's a question of water. The Hatchet borders the Piedra River just like the Rafter G does."

Dru Lee caught her lower lip between her teeth and drove silently for a time.

"Part of it is, the big outfits just don't like Dad. He's always been a loner. Wouldn't join the association Detwiler and some of the others organized to try to stop the rustling."

His eyebrows went up.

"Rustling, huh? How bad is it?"

"I haven't heard any talk about it for a while," she said. "But then, I don't do much visiting."

It was a subject which had already crossed his mind.

"Don't you ever have a chance to go anywhere? Socials, things like that? It must get pretty darned boring being stuck away out here all your life."

"I don't mind. I'm used to it."

But he heard a sigh echo behind the words.

The time had come to bring up another subject. Blondy didn't realize how thin the ice was in that direction.

"This Garrett Haley character. How long's he going to be around?"

In an instant her friendliness underwent a transformation. Kincaid could see her hands tighten on the driving lines.

"Why, I don't know. As long as he wants to."

Perversely, her sudden coolness made him push ahead.

"Yeah," he grunted. "Whether your pa wants him around or not."

Her eyes snapped.

"What is that supposed to mean?"

"It looks to me as if your pa puts up with him just because of you. Shorty doesn't care for him either. He acts like he owns the place."

In the shadow of her big hat, her face had become an angry crimson. It was too late now, though, to back up.

"Haley strikes me as nothing but a blowhard, a schemer who'd like nothing better than to get his hands on the Rafter G." He took off his hat and dipped his head in a mock bow. "I figured it was time someone told you what kind of hombre you're getting the sweets for, ma'am."

Dru Lee jerked the lines so sharply the mare threw up her head and almost came to a stop.

"It's none of your affair how I feel about Garrett Haley!" The words came through clenched teeth. "I'll thank you to mind your own business!"

She lashed the rump of the bay with the tips of the leather lines. The startled mare leaped forward, making her grab for support. A wry grin across his face, Blondy watched the buckboard bounce away along the rocky, twisting trace. Well, so much for trying to be helpful.

7

After that they traveled in silence along the road to Arrowhead. Kincaid's gaze gathered in the majestic sweep of mountains that cupped this sage-sprinkled plateau in the palm of a giant hand. On two sides of the tableland the piñon-strewn slopes shot upward toward high-country spruce and aspens, finally breaking out into a barren, wind-swept timberline.

This was the country about which Colonel Webster Buchanan had talked, back there in his fine study in Fort Worth. This was the harsh, rugged range where the Colonel had carved out a cattle empire, succeeding in the face of unforgiving elements, hostile Indians, range wars, and bitter feuds.

And just such a feud it was that had cost the Buchanans the ultimate price, a price that turned his empire to ashes in his hand. A daughter, the only child the gods of irony were to allow the Buchanans, was the sacrifice the Colonel had to make in the name of riches and power.

The set of Buchanan's features as he talked was still clear in Kincaid's mind. The white-haired old man's bearing was as regal as though he were on military parade, but the object beneath him was no spirited charger. It was a wheelchair. He had the wretched look of a lordly bull moose that has been beaten and driven from the herd by an arrogant young challenger.

"Kincaid," said he, his voice crackling like a blaze devouring dry timber, "I've saved you from hanging for one reason. There's a job I want you to do. If you carry it off, the murder warrant the sheriff is holding will be forgotten. But if you fail, I'll personally see to it that you die on the gallows."

Kincaid had measured the distance to the big double window on the second floor of the Buchanan mansion. One blow of his manacled hands would disable the aging colonel. But even if he could slip through those windows and scale the wall with his hands bound, the sheriff and his deputy, sitting there on the veranda sipping the Colonel's whiskey, would still block his flight. It would give them no little pleasure to discover Andrew Kincaid attempting to escape.

He decided to hear the Colonel out.

"Twenty years ago," said Buchanan, "I had a ranch near a place called Arrowhead, over in the territory. As fine a spread as any north of the Rio Grande. I was smart enough and tough enough to hold on in hard times, and buy out the little boys who couldn't read the signs.

"There was one man, though—a fool of a man—who wouldn't sell to me. Even when it meant starving half to death. I tried every honest means there was to get his place, but like a damned jackass, he was too stubborn. Then he had some bad luck and figured I was the cause of it. That set off the feud. And a hell of a one it was."

The Colonel leaned back in his wheelchair and looked out the window. The light sharpened his craggy features and great mane of silver hair.

"Mrs. Webster and I had a daughter. A baby she was, twenty years ago. On a day when my wife went for a drive in the buggy, with the baby in her lap, someone stampeded the horse. The buggy crashed into the river."

He paused a full half-minute.

"It was him. I know beyond any shred of doubt it was him. Trying to get even for what he imagined I had done."

Kincaid waited, his eyes on the old man's bowed head. At last Buchanan looked up.

"My wife wasn't hurt, but it cost her her sanity. Her mind no longer holds memories of it. As for me, I'm an old man now, but I can't go to my grave without settling that score. That's why I've summoned you, Kincaid. The man you killed was to have done the job for me."

"And what's that?" Blondy asked.

"Ruin the sonofabitch. Wreck the bastard. Cut him up until there's nothing left but a pile of carrion that even a buzzard wouldn't touch. You understand?"

Kincaid looked him in the eye.

"No. I'm not interested. Cold-blooded murder's not my line. Find yourself another executioner."

Buchanan spun the wheelchair about and aimed a forefinger at Kincaid.

"Don't get pious with me, young man. Not with a murder charge hanging over your head."

Blondy's eyes locked with those of the old man.

"I killed a man who was trying to kill me. That's the straight of it, whether or not your friend the sheriff wants to believe it." His words cut the air with finality. "Like I said. No deal."

Buchanan's eyes burned into him as though the older man would force acquiescence by the sheer power of his will. After a time, though, he nodded ever so slightly.

"I've thought about it. I don't want him dead. I want him left alive, to know the hell of ruin, the torment of that darkness when a man don't want to go on drawing breath."

"It won't bring your daughter back."

The Colonel turned back to the window, and Kincaid thought he saw a glistening on his cheek.

"Rebecca, her name was. The prettiest little thing you've ever seen. As pretty and bright as a star in the heavens."

The silence that followed was interminable. At last Blondy asked, "What's his name?"

The words that issued from Buchanan's throat weren't words at all, but a cry from the depths of perdition.

"Orlando Grimm!"

Their shadows were beginning to lengthen when they reached the crest of a sharp juniper-dotted ridge and gazed into the valley below. The town of Arrowhead lay in the horseshoe bend of a nondescript stream that a few miles farther on joined the Piedra River in its rolling, muddy rush toward the Rio Grande.

As they drew nearer, the urgent sounds of a busy settlement rose up to meet them. The clamor of a tipple at a hillside mine overshadowed all other sounds, as it had almost from the day a wandering prospector had stooped to pick up an Apache arrowhead and found a gold-laden outcropping of quartz at his feet. Arrowhead had quickly mushroomed into a boom town, and although the pinnacle of that growth was past, it still bore the earmarks of a vulgar, unrefined frontier metropolis. Saloons and gambling halls there were, but also evidence of respectability: a school, a church, a newspaper office, a jail, even an opera house. Stagecoach service and a telegraph line connected Arrowhead with the rest of the world, a world that didn't really care.

They left the horses in the care of an ancient, toothless Negro at the livery stable. On the boardwalk, Blondy stood and surveyed Arrowhead's main street. Dru Lee had spoken not a word since her angry outburst three hours back along the road. Kincaid had decided he wouldn't be the one to break the stalemate.

She started away along the walk, then stopped and turned.

"I would appreciate it, Mr. Kincaid, if you would arrange a room for me at the hotel. I don't care where you stay. I shall be ready to leave quite early in the morning. I trust you will have your business taken care of by then."

He looked at her until her gaze wavered. "Maybe."

She spun about and walked away, her back stiffly straight. Blondy watched, liking the litheness of her tiny waist and the angry set of her shoulders. If only she weren't Orlando Grimm's offspring.

Then he crossed the dusty street to the Saddle Horn Saloon, whose painted windows modestly proclaimed it to be "Arrowhead's Biggest and Best." Inside, he stood for a long moment, letting his eyes adjust to the dimness. It was too early in the day for the miners and the cowboys and the lumbermen and the freight haulers. Now the saloon was almost deserted. The bartender, a huge man with a bushy copper-hued mustache on his lip and a fly swatter in one hand, stood reading a month-old copy of the *Rocky Mountain*

Sentinel. At a table just inside the front door, two Mexican horse traders, their clothes crusted with trail dust, sat sipping tequila and considering the profits that would be theirs.

The only other patron of the Saddle Horn occupied a chair at a table in the far dimness, his head resting on his forearm.

"Let me have a beer," said Blondy to the bartender.

"Sure thing, amigo."

He drew the beer and slid it along the bar and immediately returned to his newspaper.

After a time, Kincaid said, "I'm looking to hire a hand. Have any idea where I might find a man?"

Reluctantly the bartender laid the paper aside.

"They come in here often enough cadging drinks. All you gotta do is wait around, I guess." He paused. "What kind of work?"

"Punching cows. Roundup. Branding."

The bartender, his bulbous nose an almost brilliant crimson, studied Kincaid for several seconds. Finally he asked, "What outfit you hirin' for?"

The question hung in the air unanswered while Blondy took a long drink of the tepid beer. He wiped his mouth with his sleeve.

"Up on the Piedra."

It was the first mystery that had come the bartender's way in a long while. His curiosity was whetted.

"Up on the Piedra, huh? And what outfit did you say it was?"

Blondy considered the question. If the Rafter G's reputation was as ill-regarded in these parts as Old Man Grimm had indicated, he'd just as soon put off answering as long as he could. But the bartender was becoming insistent. The silence was growing strained.

Kincaid became aware that someone was standing at his elbow. He felt a hand on his arm, gently. The sour odor of old whiskey stung his nostrils.

He turned and found himself looking into a pair of bloodshot eyes sunk deeply beneath heavy black brows and an unkempt mop of long black hair. The man behind the eyes could have been his own age, or twice that.

"Get lost, McHenry!" snapped the bartender, irritated that he still hadn't solved the minor riddle the blond-haired man with the wounded arm had presented him.

McHenry looked pleadingly at Kincaid.

"There ain't nobody in town I don't know. I can put you on to a cowhand or two right quick." He swallowed and licked his lips. "If you'd care to stand me to a drink."

There wasn't much likelihood that the whiskey-soak at his elbow could help, but Blondy wasn't quite ready to announce in public that he was hiring for the Rafter G. Not until he'd had a little more time to test the water.

"Bring me another beer," he said to the bartender. "And get him something."

McHenry's black-stubbled face broke into a broad smile, revealing a row of almost perfect white teeth. If, as with a horse, his teeth were any indication, the man wasn't as old as he looked, Kincaid decided.

He moved away to a table at the rear of the Saddle Horn, with McHenry following as closely as a lonely pup. Blondy sat facing the batwing doors, and the other man took a seat on his left. When the drinks came, McHenry didn't allow his shot glass to hit the tabletop. He took it from the hand of the bartender and downed it in a swallow.

"You just saved my life, pardner," he said gravely. "Another one just like that would get me over the hump."

Kincaid ignored the plea.

"You said you might know a man looking for work. How about it?"

"Sure, sure." McHenry nodded. "There's plenty around needin' work." His brows drew together as he looked into Blondy's face. "Tell you what. I'll bet you the price of a drink that the next gent who comes through them doors yonder is left-handed, just like you are. How about it? Why, you cain't hardly lose."

The intensity of McHenry's voice, the supplication in his face, made Blondy relent.

"Okay," he said. "It's a bet."

He reached to pick up his glass of beer, when a shadow fell across the doorway. As he watched, a stout barrel-chested man with a miner's squint pushed the batwings aside with his right shoulder. Beneath that shoulder was an empty sleeve, folded back and pinned at the short stub of what had been an arm.

Kincaid turned a wary look on the other man.

"How'd you manage to get so lucky?"

McHenry grinned and looked at the big clock over the mirror behind the bar.

"He comes in here every day. At the same time, to the minute."

Blondy fixed him with a reproving gaze.

"Now, what the hell would you have done if he hadn't showed up?"

McHenry closed one eye and screwed up his face.

"Made another bet. Double or nothin'."

With the second drink under his belt, McHenry's eyes began to come alive, his voice to lose its beggarly whine. The transformation was remarkable.

"Okay," said Kincaid. "Where do I find this puncher that wants to go to work?"

"Well, now," said McHenry. "What's the job?"

"Roundup."

"I can sit a saddle and dab a rope on an ol' calf," the black-haired man said matter-of-factly.

"Where's the last place you worked?"

"Over in the Panhandle. The Seven-Fork."

"How come you to quit?"

"Got drunk and burned down a line shack. And six sections of pasture. The ramrod run me off."

Kincaid regarded him silently for a time. Whatever else he might be, McHenry appeared honest enough.

"Suits me if it suits you," he said. "I'll pick you up in the morning on the way back to the headquarters."

It was an afterthought. McHenry asked, "What outfit did you say?"

"Up on the Piedra. The Rafter G."

McHenry, now that he was no longer unemployed, was in the act of signaling to the bartender for another whiskey when he heard the words. His head snapped around.

"The Rafter G? Are you loco? There ain't no self-respectin' cowpuncher in the whole territory that would sign on with Old Man Grimm."

He suddenly realized he had indicted the man sitting across the table.

"Well, what I mean is, the Rafter G's name ain't exactly lily-white, mister."

Kincaid leveled a cold gaze on the other man.

"And what's wrong with the Rafter G?"

McHenry ducked his head and studied the bottom of the empty whiskey glass before him.

"Aw, I didn't mean nothin'. A man can hear all kinds of stories. . . ."

His voice trailed off. He was obviously wishing he hadn't opened the subject.

"Let's have it." Kincaid's voice was hard. "What the hell is it about the Rafter G that makes everybody in the territory as skittish as an old maid at a shivaree? Spit it out."

McHenry started to stand. Blondy's hand shot out across the little table and grabbed a handful of shirtfront.

"Sit down. You're not through talking."

He released the shirt and hooked a quick

finger in the bartender's direction. McHenry downed the glass of amber fire with almost as much urgency as he had the first. When he spoke, his eyes still refused to meet Kincaid's.

"The story is that Old Man Grimm ain't beyond puttin' his brand on somebody else's cow. Leastways, that's the tale the boys from the Hatchet outfit keep spreadin'. I ain't sayin' it's true."

Blondy's voice was low, steady, and knife-edged.

"If I was a gent who cared anything for his skin, I sure wouldn't make it a habit to go around accusing someone of rustling. That could damned well cause a man's health to go bad."

McHenry looked up, and for the first time Blondy saw grit behind the dark bloodshot eyes.

"You insisted on knowin', friend."

He slid his chair back from the table.

"I'm gonna have to owe you that last drink. I'm much obliged."

The hinges on the batwing doors squealed inward. Kincaid glanced up, but all he could see were the silhouettes of three men against the bright sunlight of the street outside. He had turned back to McHenry when he heard a voice he'd heard before.

"Well, looka here," came the words from the bar. "If it ain't the bootlicker that's throwed in with Old Man Grimm!"

8

Kincaid's head came about. Lined up along the long, shiny mahogany rail were three cowboys, each with a Colt slung low on a hip. Two of them were strangers to Blondy. The third was Luke Nabours.

Now Nabours stood with his back to the bar, his elbows hooked over its curled edge. He spat a brown trail of tobacco juice in the general direction of a brass spittoon on the floor and drew a sleeve across his bearded jaw.

"Boys," he said to the air around him. "What's the one thing that smells worse than a sheep? I'll tell you what. It's a gent that'll ride for the Rafter G."

Luke's two companions guffawed. They had caught the drift of Nabours' talk.

Kincaid turned back to McHenry.

"I know the loudmouth that's doing the talking. Who are the two with him?"

"Them's Hatchet riders," said McHenry. "Slick Detwiler's boys. You shore know how to pick yore friends."

"Yeah," Blondy muttered, watching Nabours down a half-glass of whiskey. The man must have made straight for Detwiler's spread when he left the Rafter G on the run. It began to add up in Kincaid's mind. Nabours still owed him that thousand dollars taken from his money belt. And a betting man sure might lay odds it was Nabours who had shot the front legs out from under Blondy's sorrel horse.

Nabours wasn't through talking.

"Yeah, I can tell you about the Rafter G," he said, looking straight at Kincaid. "Nothin' but a pack of thievin' coyotes. The whole bunch of 'em ought to be strung up with a new rope, starting with Old Man Grimm."

Blondy felt the old tightening in his gut. His scalp tingled. Every sight and sound in the dimness of the bar grew crisp and sharp. Looking into his face, McHenry was startled to see a half-smile on his lips.

Slowly, deliberately, Kincaid pushed his chair back and rose to his feet. At the bar, Nabours' two companions had drifted out and now stood flanking him, gun hands low.

But the bartender was an old hand. He

could read these signs with less difficulty than he could read the print on his newspaper. Now he laid the paper on the mahogany and slipped one hand out of sight beneath it. His words weren't loud, but they seemed so in the stillness.

"Not in my saloon, you don't. I'm gonna scatter gun the first hombre that reaches for a Colt's in here." He inclined his head in a spare nod. "You'll find the street right outside them doors."

The half-smile was still on Kincaid's face as he looked toward Nabours.

"You've run up a pretty fair account, amigo," he said evenly. "You've got a thousand dollars that belongs to me, you've accused the outfit I work for of rustling, and I'm betting you're the jasper that shot my horse out from under me up there on the Piedra River. What do you say we drift along outside and get on with our business?"

Luke felt his confidence suddenly begin to waver. Sure, he was fast with a Colt, as fast as the next man. But the tall, slim cowboy across the room from him was too cool, too steady. He gritted his teeth and shot a quick glance toward his two companions, and then felt his mettle returning. They'd know what to do.

Cautiously they moved outside, all of them, where the late-afternoon sun had painted the buildings and storefronts and street dust with a golden haze.

Aware of a stiffness that lingered in his wounded shoulder, Kincaid moved out to the middle of Arrowhead's main street. He got no pleasure from what he was about to do, but he had no doubt about his ability to do it.

He watched Luke Nabours talk intently for a moment with the two Hatchet cowboys, then saunter out into the dust and turn to face him thirty paces away.

But in the act of turning, Nabours' hand streaked toward his gun. It was only a fraction of a second's edge, but Luke wanted any edge he could get, even with two companions backing his play.

The little knot of men on the walk in front of the Saddle Horn Saloon didn't see Kincaid's hand move. What they did see was an ivory-handled Colt bucking in his left hand. A frown, like a quick shadow, touched Nabours' face. He seemed to be studying the ground five or six feet in front of him. Finally his own gun fired, the bullet kicking dust onto his boots.

He fell forward, sliding on his face until his body lay full-length in the street. His hat rolled on its brim, out of reach. But Luke Nabours was beyond caring.

Blondy knew where his bullet had gone and he had already shifted his gaze toward the men on the boardwalk before Nabours' heart stopped beating.

But the two Hatchet riders were standing in a strangely frozen posture, each with his hand at a careful distance from the butt of his six-gun. A moment later the reason for their irresolution became clear. McHenry, the drunk, was leaning on his elbows on the hitching rack at the street's edge. In his hand was an old Army .44, not pointing at anything in particular. But it was clear enough that the two Hatchet cowboys had gotten his message.

There was movement from the stores and buildings toward the man lying in the street. Kincaid walked over, stooped down, and slid a fat leather pouch from Nabours' hip pocket. The bulge in it told Blondy that most of his thousand dollars was still there.

The crowd around the dead man parted. Through the opening came a hurrying, heavy-set man breathing noisily around a thicket of mustache, black and bristly. On his vest was a worn star.

"I'll take that!" he barked, and grabbed the

leather pouch from Blondy's hand. With the other he snatched the gun from his hip and held its muzzle against Kincaid's belly. "You're under arrest, boy. Murder ain't allowed in my town."

Kincaid looked about him. In the crowd that had gathered there wasn't a sympathetic face. Most looked as though they'd be perfectly happy to see another killing. The hanging of one Blondy Kincaid, for instance. For a sliver of a moment he debated about disabling the sheriff and taking it on the run. He could do it. But it probably would mean killing the stout lawman.

Kincaid surrendered his gun to the sheriff, who drew a pair of shackles from his hip pocket and clamped them roughly about his wrists. It was Sheriff Lew Dollarhide's show, and he didn't want to disappoint his audience.

The sheriff's office and jail were only a short distance away, but they gathered new onlookers as they walked. An even dozen boy-age youths skipped ahead, clearing their path to the calaboose.

Blondy watched the sheriff lock the barred door of the cell.

"It was a fair fight, Sheriff. Ask anyone who saw it."

Dollarhide glanced up, then looked quickly

back to the key in his hand.

"Well, now. That's something the circuit judge will have to decide, boy. Arrowhead is a civilized town. Killin' ain't allowed."

"When's the judge due?"

The sheriff grinned a humorless grin.

"He was here a couple of days back. It'll be a month or better before he comes up from Socorro again. But don't you go gettin' anxious about missin' his visit. You'll be right here."

Sheriff Dollarhide turned on his heel and walked away, the ring of big keys jangling against his leg.

"Damn!" muttered Blondy. He backed up and sank to the edge of the single bunk and swore again. He wasn't going to help Colonel Buchanan's cause, or his own, sitting on his hands in a jail cell. He might as well have stayed in the Fort Worth lockup.

The sun was down and twilight had given way to darkness when he heard the sounds of boot heels on the wooden floor. The sheriff came in carrying a coal-oil lamp above his head. Behind him was the shaggy-haired McHenry.

"You've got five minutes," said the lawman. He set the lamp on a shelf against the wall and departed.

McHenry leaned against the barred cell door and deliberately rolled a cigarette. He lighted it from the lamp and turned to face Kincaid.

"Does that offer of a job still stand?"

Blondy regarded him for a long moment, then nodded.

McHenry let the smoke roll from his nose.

"I've decided I like the odds. Now, here's my idea. I don't have a horse, but I'll get yours. After midnight sometime. Then I'll tie a rope around a couple of bars of that window there. This old adobe jail can't be too tough."

For the first time since he'd looked up and seen the sheriff coming at him, Kincaid felt a glimmer of hope. One friend, even a sot like McHenry, was a way yonder better than none at all when a man was caught in a real bind.

Blondy shook his head.

"Huh-uh. That wouldn't solve a thing. Tell you what. You go over to the hotel and locate Orlando Grimm's daughter. Name's Dru Lee. She's about this tall and kinda skinny. Little short nose, with freckles. Tell her to get herself over here to the jail. Pronto."

Doubts began to assail Kincaid after McHenry's departure. Dru Lee probably would simply refuse to come to the jail. Even if she did, what could she do to help a man the sheriff had locked up on a murder charge? Blondy gripped the steel bars of the cell and cursed the names of Orlando Grimm and Webster Buchanan, and his own.

Dru Lee came, though. By the light of the lamp she looked through the barred door at Kincaid and stamped her booted foot on the puncheon floor.

"You idiot!" But her woman's voice sounded fragile and out of place in the prison. "Dad needs every hand he can get, and you've got to go and get yourself thrown in jail. What in heaven's name did you do?"

In spite of himself, Blondy felt himself turning red under her accusing gaze.

"Didn't McHenry tell you?"

"I didn't hear his name. But, no. He didn't tell me. He just said the sheriff had locked you up. I started not to come."

"Well, thanks," he said sardonically.

"Don't thank me. I didn't do it for you." She paused to catch her breath. "Are you going to tell me why you're in this place?"

"I got into a little scrap."

"I'm not surprised," she said.

"I killed Luke Nabours."

The intake of her breath was a faint little-girl's cry in the dimness. Blondy remembered the shock in her face when she had looked at the body of Skew lying on the floor of the ranch house.

"Why?" Her hand was up against her throat.

"He'd thrown in with Slick Detwiler. Came in with a couple of Hatchet hands. Started ridin' me."

"You didn't have to start a fight. You could have ignored him."

Her words and the tone of her voice, and the fact that he had to look at her through the bars of a cell door, triggered a sudden anger.

"I'll try to explain," he said, making only a small effort to mask the irritation in his voice. "Along with a few other choice remarks, Nabours all but accused the Rafter G of rustling Hatchet cows. You may not be able to understand it, but no man with an ounce of guts is going to stand there and take that kind of talk. Savvy?"

His words were hard and brittle. Dru Lee backed up a step and avoided his eyes. Ever since this tall cowboy had come to the Rafter G, he'd done nothing but cause her frustration. Every time they talked, it became an argument. Why didn't she just turn and walk away and leave him locked up in Arrowhead's jail?

"I'll see what I can do," she said.

The town was already asleep when they left it behind, Blondy astride the big palomino and McHenry driving the buckboard, with Dru Lee on the seat beside him.

Kincaid's curiosity finally overcame him.

"How did you manage it?"

"I went to see Sam Flowers. The banker." She didn't look at him, but kept her face toward the quarter-moon emerging over the mountains to the east. "You'll have to come back to town when the circuit judge gets here."

"I'm beholden to you, ma'am," Blondy said.

"Thank Dad. It's his money."

Daylight reached the Rafter G headquarters at the same time they did. Dru Lee went straight to the house to start breakfast. Blondy and McHenry unsaddled and unharnessed. Shorty and Chorizo had already caught up their mounts.

The bowlegged little foreman sat on the top rail of the corral fence and watched the two at work. Finally he spat the yield from his cud of tobacco into the dirt.

"What's he doin' here?" he demanded, nodding in the direction of McHenry, who was carrying the armload of harness into the shed.

"I hired him," Kincaid said.

"You hired that wuthless soak! I know him. He ain't done an honest day's work in years." He spat again, with feeling. "Knowed I should have gone and done it myself."

Kincaid's humor was drawn too thin.

"He pulled me out of a tight. If I see you giving him a hard time, I'll jerk them whiskers out of your jaw. One at a time."

Shorty's face swelled. He started to speak, but choked on tobacco juice. Blondy turned his back and walked to the house.

9

Orlando Grimm was sitting on his pillow in a chair at the kitchen table. His face had all the serenity of a mountain storm.

"What happened in town!" The words were a thunderclap.

"Didn't she tell you?" Blondy asked.

"Wouldn't tell me nothin'. Except that you hired that drunk McHenry. That's what I get. Sendin' a boy to do a man's job."

Kincaid's irritation hadn't fully subsided from Shorty's critical observation. He turned on the old man sitting at the table.

"The Rafter G has to take anybody it can get. And you damned well know why. Because the whole country believes you're swinging a wide loop."

The coffee cup in Grimm's hand began to shake. He looked quickly toward the door to the bedroom where Dru Lee had gone a moment earlier.

"That's a damned dirty lie! That's the story that snake Detwiler has spread, tryin' to ruin me. I ain't never put a brand on a critter that wasn't rightfully mine. You just keep your mouth shut about it, boy. I won't have that girl frettin' because of something some low-down piece of trash like Detwiler has to say."

Kincaid's jaw was set.

"It doesn't really make a whole hell of a lot of difference whether it's the truth or a lie when some hombre makes the accusation right out in public."

"What's that supposed to signify?"

"It means Luke Nabours went straight to the Hatchet outfit when he left here. And he's the gent that was running off at the mouth about you stealing livestock."

Grimm struggled to get to his feet, but the pain in his hip jerked him back to the chair.

"That good-for-nothin' polecat! If he's gone over to Detwiler, he's found the right crowd to run with. Addin' some more lies to them the Hatchet outfit is always spreadin'."

Blondy ran his knuckles along the day's growth of stubble on his jaw.

"He plumb got over telling lies."

"Yeah? How come?"

"I killed him."

The words struck Grimm speechless. He

opened his mouth to speak, then closed it. Finally he hit the tabletop a blow with the flat of his hand that resounded like a pistol shot.

"Are you tellin' it square?"

Kincaid's eyes were hard.

"That's right. He called me out, with two Hatchet hands to back his play. McHenry convinced 'em they oughtn't to interfere."

"Well. What happened to Nabours?"

"He had an idea he was pretty fast with that Colt's of his."

"He was."

Kincaid shrugged.

The door to the bedroom swung open then, and Dru Lee came in, tucking a strand of hair in place.

"Girl," said Grimm, his tone changing suddenly from harsh inquisition to gentleness, "is he shootin' straight with me? About Nabours?"

She stopped beside the cupboard and looked directly at Kincaid. He couldn't be sure of the emotion in her eyes. Affection it was not, however.

"Yes, Dad. I didn't see it. But Sheriff Dollarhide locked him up."

The mention of the sheriff's name set Grimm to muttering.

"Owned lock, stock, and barrel by Detwiler. Somebody ought to take that badge and . . ."

Abruptly he stopped and speared Blondy with his dark eyes.

"How the devil did you get out of jail?"

Kincaid leaned against the door facing, a look of casual interest on his face. Hell was fixing to break loose in the room.

"I put up his bond," Dru Lee said quietly.

It was the first time Kincaid had heard anything resembling apprehension in her voice.

"How much? How much?" Grimm breathed the question.

"One thousand, five hundred dollars."

"One thousand, five hundred dollars?" The words lodged in his throat. He jerked to his feet, the pain in his wounded buttock forgotten. "Fifteen hundred dollars! There ain't no man alive worth puttin' up that much money for. Have you gone plumb loco, girl?"

Blondy saw her jaw tighten. She was afraid of the old man, but not much.

"The ranch needs every man it can get."

Blondy frowned, irritated at himself. Why should he give a tinker's damn if it was for the ranch, rather than for Blondy Kincaid, that she'd managed to get him free?

"Where'd you get that kind of money?" Grimm barked.

"I borrowed it."

"From that old skinflint Sam Flowers, I reckon." His face was growing livid again, the big vein on his forehead swelling to prominence. "He's probably already licking his chops over the interest he's gonna nail me for."

He groaned and sat back down. Both hands were on the table, drawn into tight fists. Orlando Grimm wanted desperately to vent his rage on someone, but he couldn't bring himself to aim it at his daughter. She was immune from his wrath. Kincaid started to grin, until Grimm turned toward him, ignoring the entrance of Shorty and Chorizo and McHenry.

"Boy." His voice had the delicacy of an unoiled wagon wheel. "I don't think the Rafter G can afford the likes of you, but I'm going to get every cent back if I have to take it out in blood. Get your gear together. You're going to a line shack so far back in the hills you won't even think about causin' trouble. Or costin' me money."

The word brought new pain to his eyes. He grimaced and turned to the foreman.

"Shorty, this miserable excuse for a cowboy will ride out to that Purgatory Canyon country. There's livestock in there we haven't seen in three or four years."

Shorty was pouring himself a cup of coffee.

"Hell, boss, It'll take one man a month of Sundays to work that Purgatory country."

"He'll do it. And in a lot less time than a month," the rancher growled. "You and the boys will have your hands full gettin' the pens in shape and roundin' up everything along the river canyon."

The meal was eaten in silence. From time to time a groan would issue from Grimm's throat. Blondy knew it wasn't the hip wound that caused his agony.

Not much later, Kincaid had his palomino saddled and the big bay gelding caught up on a lead rope, a grub sack slung across his withers. Shorty worked a plug of tobacco from his hip pocket and worried off another chew.

"Up yonder," he said, pointing toward an immense breastwork of mountains poking holes in the western sky. "Head toward them two biggest peaks, the two that look like a pair of tits. Purgatory Canyon runs smack dab into 'em."

Kincaid's forehead wrinkled into a frown.

"That's in the direction of Detwiler's spread. If I'm in his backyard dodging slugs, I won't have much time for poppin' brush looking for Rafter G livestock."

Shorty shook his head.

"The Hatchet is on the other side of that line of peaks. Detwiler's boys don't drift over this way, and we stay clear of his country."

He grunted and spat, the brown stain spreading into his graying whiskers.

"If you do catch sight of any of them Hatchet boys, watch out for a gent they call Alamo Sam. He's the ramrod. Got a disposition about as sweet as a rattlesnake. And a gun hand that's twice as sudden."

The palomino was anxious to cover ground. A quarter-mile from the ranch house, Blondy turned and looked back, and was surprised to see a figure standing by the clothesline. It was Dru Lee, shading her eyes against the sun and watching him ride away. He grinned, not really knowing why. An instant later he uttered an oath and spurred the stud into a lope. The arrogant face of Garrett Haley had intruded, unbidden, upon his thoughts.

Kincaid was following a steep ridge that grew into the sharp shoulder of a mountain and continued upward toward the inhospitable heights of the Rocky Mountains in the distance. He could feel a decided drop in the temperature as his horse labored upward. He left behind a broad plateau of pungent silver-grey sagebrush, cut through a belt of piñon trees, and rode into a forest of blackjack pines. Blue jays scolded the two-and four-legged intruders. More than once Kincaid spotted mule deer, singly and in small herds, moving warily through the forested slopes.

Terrain that from a distance had appeared relatively smooth and unbroken had suddenly become a fragmented world standing on its edge. Mountains shot upward to incredible heights, ending in ragged spires of stone against the azure sky. High-elevation trees, wind-whipped spruce and firs, struggled to stand sensibly upright on canyon walls that tilted foolishly at sheer angles.

It was hellish country, Kincaid conceded as the palomino stallion and the gelding fought their way up an impossible slope. Aloud, for the benefit of the stallion's alert ears, he cursed Orlando Grimm with painstaking thoroughness.

"The cantankerous old penny pincher ought to be horsewhipped on general principles," he told the horse. "It'll be a waste of time even trying to get a look at cattle in this piece of hades, let alone trying to gather and drive them anywhere."

He grunted another oath as the stallion lost his footing and slid halfway to the bottom of a sheer cutbank. Orlando Grimm's temperament was fitting counterpart to the devilish badlands they called the Purgatory: cruel, ruthless, and unforgiving. It was no wonder Colonel Webster Buchanan had had a running feud with the old codger. Or that any of Grimm's neighbors had the problem. His own mother must have been hard put to love such a character, Blondy mused.

But the girl. Ah, there was a different matter. She had moments of temper, like her father, but there was a subtle refinement in her being that contravened the coarseness of the old man. He shook his head. No one but Mother Nature could have created an object of such delicacy from a sow's ear.

The Purgatory Peaks were still a dark outline in the distance when the sun slipped through their cleavage. Blackness settled into the depths of the canyon with a suddenness that almost caught Blondy unawares. He made camp on a meager shelf along the canyon wall, had a quick meal of beans, tortillas, and coffee, and was asleep the instant he settled into his bedroll.

In the early afternoon of the next day he found the cabin, all but hidden in a copse of bristlecone pine and timberline spruce. No human had set foot in the little house in several seasons. Daylight filtered through the roof. Pack rats, hardly concerned at his presence, scurried across the dirt floor carrying little treasures.

A blackened stone fireplace occupied one end of the tiny room, and to another wall clung an uncertain bunk, its rawhide lashings offering no guarantees.

Kincaid constructed a pine-needle broom, swept out the line shack, and unloaded his gear from the bay. Afterward, he stood for a long time in the doorway of the log cabin, surveying the panorama that stretched before him. In the late-afternoon sun it was a world of sharp peaks and jagged ridges that swept away into a deepening purple haze, turning all the sawtooth edges into velvet softness.

Blondy grunted a satisfied grunt as he fashioned a cigarette. Consigning him to the loneliness of Purgatory Canyon, Grimm had supposed it would be a harsh and disagreeable indenture. He grinned, remembering winters he had spent in line camps, seasons when he would see no other human being from late autumn until the ice began to thin on mountain lakes in the spring. It was his kind of life.

But Shorty had been right about one thing. Gathering cattle in the Purgatory was about as practical as grabbing cutthroat trout from a stream by hand. At the end of the first day, Kincaid had one lone cow and her calf penned in the pole corral at the head of the meadow, a quarter-mile downslope from the cabin. It wasn't that he hadn't been able to catch sight of the critters, but driving a badlands veteran out of a tangle of scrub cedars and shinnery was sheer frustration for a cowboy, murder on a good horse, and hardly more than entertainment for the cow.

On the second day, Blondy changed his approach, reverting to the practice he'd learned as a brush cowboy in Texas' Big Thicket country. Instead of trying to drive the wild-eyed brutes to the pole corral, he began roping them and, one at a time, dragging them to the enclosure in the meadow.

The strategy had its drawbacks. Once an old mossy-horned steer with a great raw wound running from shoulder to flank turned on him and charged. Blondy was trying to decide if the claw mark was mountain lion or grizzly and barely spurred the bay gelding out of the angry steer's path in time.

It was on the fifth day, with a respectable number of cattle corralled in the meadow, that Kincaid shifted his search for strays westward, toward the stone-rimmed rampart that marked the dividing line between the range claimed by the Rafter G and that wearing Slick Detwiler's Hatchet brand.

If anything, the country was more rugged, the canyons steeper and deeper, the undergrowth thicker than the mountainsides he'd been working. The morning had been unfruitful. He had seen a half-dozen animals, but all had vanished in the brush before he could shake out a loop.

He reined the palomino up in a patch of mountain muhly grass and dismounted. Hunkered down with his back to a wind-twisted cedar, Kincaid built a cigarette and gazed across the canyon that dropped away at his feet. Beyond it were the twin peaks Shorty had pointed out to him, their shoulders still bearing signs of last winter's snows.

Directly across the canyon and on a level with his own position, a movement registered on Blondy's senses. The afternoon sun was squarely in his eyes, but a few moments later he saw it again, a tawny, fluid motion along an outcropping of stone on the opposite canyon wall. A cougar! The hair along the back of his neck stiffened. It was a female on the hunt. Trailing behind her were two balls of tan fur, a pair of kittens, barely visible from Kincaid's vantage point.

Quickly he slid the .44-40 Winchester from its boot on the saddle and laid the long barrel of the rifle across the root end of a downed tree. There she was, crouched low against the stone ledge as though expecting her prey to emerge on the trail below her. The kittens, sensing that the game had become earnest, had disappeared among the trees.

Blondy muttered a halfhearted curse. It was five hundred yards if it was a foot to where the big cat crouched, twice the effective range of the rifle in his hand. Remembering the great wound along the ribs of the enraged steer he had dodged a couple of days earlier, he was ready to bet the female catamount across the canyon was the cause of that wound. But all he could do from this distance was watch.

Suddenly on the thin, clear mountain air came a sound to his ear, the sound of a hoof turning over a stone. The reason for the cat's wariness became clear. An animal was on the trail below her and headed for disaster.

A moment later he saw movement through the trees that bordered the game trail. The animal, whatever it was, lacked the usual hunted beast's survival instincts.

Then, a half-dozen steps before reaching the cougar's covert, the quarry came into

Kincaid's view. It was a paint horse, head down and picking its cautious way along the narrow, rocky trail. The paint's rider was doing the same, watching the trail as though to lend aid to the horse's senses.

The sequence of events that followed consumed only a few seconds. Powerless to help, Blondy could only watch.

The big cat, suddenly aware of the human astride the horse, decided against attack. Instead, she fell back, spitting and snarling and clawing the air before vanishing up the mountainside. It was enough, though, to send the paint horse into a crazed frenzy. He reared and spun about, crashing away through the trees beside the trail. In a flicker of movement, Blondy saw the rider snatched from the saddle by the thigh-thick branch of a massive pine tree.

10

It took Kincaid the better part of an hour to circle the sheer chasm and climb the far slope. The palomino's sides were heaving when they came at last to the ledge where the cougar had been poised to leap.

Although the last hint of daylight was still clinging to the uppermost peaks, the canyons were already in deep shadow. Kincaid swore tiredly. It was going to be difficult enough to fetch the horseman out of the depths of the canyon without having to do it in the dark. If he was still alive.

He spurred the stallion along the narrow trail, searching for the point at which the paint had spun about and stampeded away through the trees. But shale covered the mountainside. Only an overturned stone here and there gave evidence of the frightened horse's passage. And beside the trail, the slope dropped away precipitously. How the bolting animal had kept from tumbling down the incline was a marvel in itself.

At last he found the big pine. He tied the palomino, took his lariat down from the saddle, and carefully began to work his way down the hillside. The footing was treacherous. When he could no longer be certain of keeping his feet under him, he made one end of the rope fast to a small tree and began to let himself down hand over hand.

He saw the figure in the dimness then, lying facedown across a ledge of stone that broke the near-vertical face of the mountain. The lariat was barely long enough. Bracing his feet carefully, Kincaid worked his way down until he could stand on the narrow outcropping.

"It sure as hell would simplify things if this hombre was dead," he breathed to himself, glancing beyond the ledge to the black emptiness below.

With one hand grasping the rope's end, he knelt and caught up a limp wrist. Astonishment caused him to grunt aloud. The arm he held was slender and soft, the hand delicately tapered.

"I'll be damned!"

He caught one shoulder and gently turned her onto her back. She was either unconscious or dead, and Blondy quickly saw the reason. The big limb of the ponderosa had struck her squarely across the forehead. An angry redness had spread from the line of her raven-black hair to the bridge of her nose. Her face had already begun to swell, distorting her features. A tiny trickle of blood had drawn a zigzag line across one cheek.

What in tarnation's name would a woman be doing riding through these mountains? She hadn't been traveling far. The horse had carried no saddlebags, no supplies. And women didn't do that sort of thing anyway. She had to've come from a ranch somewhere in the region, he concluded. But that was no help now. It was the next thing to pitch black in the canyon, and hanging by his fingernails all night on a ledge of rock no bigger than a saddle blanket wasn't his idea of a good time.

He shifted his grip on the rope to his right hand and caught her around the waist, hitching the soft, limp body along his arm until she lay across his shoulder. Then he started up.

The sheer slope, strewn with shale, afforded scant purchase for his booted feet. Slowly, inching along the rope, Blondy worked his way up the mountain. His wounded shoulder was aflame with pain by the time he reached the level where he had tied the stallion.

He placed the woman on a mattress of pine needles and studied her face in the muted light. She might have been good-looking, and then again, she might not. It was impossible to tell with the puffiness that was swelling into a purple goose egg across her eyes, nose, and forehead.

He found a pulse in her wrist, a weak, fluttery kind of heartbeat that told him the blow was more than just a knockout punch. She needed quiet and a warm bed, and as far as Kincaid knew, the line shack was the only one within a day's ride. He lifted her to the saddle, straddled the palomino behind her swaying form, and sent the horse forward into the near-darkness of Purgatory Canyon.

A sliver of moon made its appearance before he had traveled far, but it was still toward the tag end of the night when he reached the cabin, cold and stiff and wondering if the woman was still alive. He laid her on the bunk, covered her with his blankets, and built up a pine-knot fire in the fireplace.

By the light of the candle he examined her again. Still alive, he decided, but hardly more than that. He bathed her badly swollen forehead with icy water from the spring below the cabin, tucked the blankets in closely around her, and set about fixing breakfast. He still had a job to do for Orlando Grimm. Or, more precisely, for Colonel Webster Buchanan. With a start, Blondy realized it had been days since he had given any thought to his real purpose at the Rafter G. That mission was to pull the linchpin on Grimm, to destroy him as thoroughly as Grimm himself had destroyed the dream of the Webster Buchanans two decades in the past.

Kincaid sat in the doorway and rolled a cigarette while the sun burst over the horizon like some gigantic creature giving birth to a golden orb, alive with flame—the same sun that had looked down on the Colonel and a bride hardly half his age when they had come to build a cattle empire. There were no children to distract him from his goal, not until he had amassed the greater part of his wealth.

When the baby came, the Colonel had already lived a half-century. Rebecca was her name, he had said worshipfully. And Buchanan was ready then to become a benevolent man, a good neighbor. But the time for that had run out. The die was cast. The ranchers who had felt his ruthlessness, his callous disdain for fairness in business dealings, lay scattered across the territory like the hulks of wrecked ships caught on a hidden reef.

One of them was Orlando Grimm.

Buchanan had made no apologies for what he called smart business. He had admitted to Kincaid while he sat imprisoned in his wheelchair in the plush surroundings of a haunted mansion that he had given no quarter in his quest for riches. And, yes, Orlando Grimm had served as one rung in his ladder upward. Nothing outside the law, mind you. Buchanan was a law-abiding man. But there were ways and ways to suck a man's blood without stepping across that fine line.

The white-haired old man had chuckled humorlessly at a recollection. Then, curling his dry, bony fingers in his lap and looking for all the world like a vulture gazing down from a dead tree limb, as much for himself as for the tall blond-haired man across the room, the Colonel had relived the episode.

There was a stretch of river ground that Buchanan wanted very badly, a broad sweep of canyon bottom called Beaver Meadows, but Grimm had claimed it because it was a logical extension of his range rights.

Colonel Buchanan offered to buy that stretch of river and its grassy meadows, but Grimm wouldn't listen to reason. He didn't know the man he was up against, though. When Webster Buchanan made up his mind that he was going to have something, the devil himself would be hard put to head him off. He bought six cases of dynamite, gathered a crew of Mexicans, and rode a day's distance upstream along the Piedra.

It was not long after that when an astonished Orlando Grimm discovered that his rich stretch of river meadows had all but dried up. He straightaway sought out the Colonel.

"Buchanan," said Grimm. "I've got more range than I can decently use. I've decided to let you have them Beaver Meadows at your price. That was seven thousand dollars, as I recollect."

The Colonel stood on the top step of his porch and gazed above Grimm's head into the distance, where the Purgatory Peaks shone gold in the waning afternoon.

"I don't know that I really want those meadows, Grimm. Perhaps you should hang on to them." He shrugged. "Tell you what. If you're dead set on selling, I'll give you an even thousand and hope you don't accept my offer."

Grimm took the money and rode away, cursing mightily.

Two days later, the Piedra was running bank-full again.

As the Colonel's story unfolded, back there in his fine Fort Worth manor, Kincaid had begun to feel a certain sympathy for any man unlucky enough to find himself an enemy of Webster Buchanan. But the old man's narrative didn't end there. He had to tell the rest of it, as though the telling would assuage the agony in his breast. Detail by detail, he related to Blondy how his infant daughter had met her death, and how the loss had destroyed his wife's mind.

When he came to the end of the story, he was weeping unashamedly, the cries of a child. It was then that Blondy had made his bargain with the Colonel, the bargain that brought him to the Rafter G. It was the destruction of Orlando Grimm that he had pledged to Buchanan, in exchange for his own freedom.

Kincaid's musings were interrupted by a moan from the bunk a few steps away. He went over and looked down at the woman, feeling a helplessness that was foreign to his nature. Her pulse was stronger now, but there was still no response to his voice, to the pressure of his hand on her wrist. She might lie there unconscious for days, and he didn't dare leave her long enough to make the two-day trip to the Rafter G. He swore. Leaving her even long enough to spend a few hours chousing Grimm's mountain-wild cattle out of the brush was out of the question.

He bathed the great bruise across her forehead once more, and studied her figure beneath the blanket. Her blouse and pants and boots were of top-grade material, probably tailored expressly for her. About her neck was a heavy gold necklace set with precious stones. Clearly this woman wasn't a wandering gypsy. She belonged in a good home.

Along one side, just above her waist, bright red blood had seeped through her blouse. He had failed to notice it. Reluctantly he unbuttoned the garment, his face growing crimson at the act circumstances had forced on him. Gently he pulled the cloth aside and saw that the flesh below her rib cage was torn in a deep, angry slash. It would have to be washed clean.

He left her lying there and took up the wooden bucket, heading for the tiny spring a hundred yards down the slope.

Kincaid's thoughts stayed with the woman. Without conscious direction, his mind strayed away on a trail of its own choosing, comparing her with that other one, that Dru Lee Grimm. The stranger lying up there on his bunk had a ripeness, a woman's fullness, that Grimm's daughter was a long way from attaining. That stubborn filly was still nothing more than a freckle-faced tomboy, although she had ambitions of convincing Garrett Haley otherwise. Somebody needed to teach her a lesson or two.

He was squatting beside the meager trickle of water with his mind two days away when he heard a quick, soft movement through the air behind him. The warning came too late. He was jerked backward, his arms pinned against his sides. The noose of a lariat had dropped around him with the stealth and finality of a striking snake.

11

Two more quick turns of the rope around his body left Blondy powerless to move a hand. He felt his Colt being lifted from its holster. He had been taken as easily as an old woman.

He turned and looked into the eyes of the two men who had stood along the street in Arrowhead and witnessed the fatal settling of accounts between him and Luke Nabours.

"Well, well, well." One of the cowboys grinned, his lips drawn back to reveal a broken line of tobacco-stained teeth. "If it ain't Old Man Grimm's hotshot gunslinger. Looka here, Red. He don't look so all-fired mean now, does he?"

Red reached out and grabbed Kincaid's shirtfront.

"All right, you smart bastard. I've a half-notion to beat your brains out right here with my fists. I'd do it, too, if Alamo didn't want the pleasure hisself."

Sick to his stomach at his own negligence, Blondy stumbled up the hill ahead of his two captors, one holding the end of the lariat that pinioned his arms and the other pressing the muzzle of a .44 Colt against his ear.

A mustachioed cowboy, scarecrow thin and stooped at the shoulders, came through the doorway of the cabin, saw the trio laboring up the slope, and poked his head back inside.

"Hey, Alamo. Come on out and have yourself a look."

The first feature of Alamo Sam to come through the doorway was a boot like none Blondy had seen before. Calfskin, black and white, with the hair still on. Inlaid with gold and silver, and propped up on heels of ludicrous height. Looking down into the face of the little man before him, Kincaid suddenly wanted to chuckle. He had envisioned a big man, a man hewn from a tall oak, not a sawed-off runt on stilts.

But he looked again into the washed-out blue eyes of the little man and felt a chill along his spine. This undersized piece of raw meat hadn't won his reputation as a gunfighter, nor his job as ramrod of the Hatchet outfit, by standing around with his thumb up his nose while folks made jokes about his size.

Alamo Sam dipped the tall crown of his beaverskin hat toward Kincaid and looked toward Red. He didn't bother to voice the question.

"Yeah, he's the polecat me and Wilbanks was tellin' you about, Alamo," Red said quickly. "The one that gunned down Luke Nabours over at Arrowhead. The Rafter G man!"

The final words had the raw sound of an oath.

Alamo Sam turned his gaze back to Kincaid. His faded eyes were flat, without expression.

"What's she doing here?"

Blondy's eyes locked with those of the Hatchet ramrod.

"I brought her here."

The brows of the Hatchet foreman drew down until his eyes were narrow slits.

"She's bad hurt."

"I'd say so."

Alamo Sam's temper was crowding the surface, like a volcano approaching eruption.

"How did it happen, cowboy? You better pray you've got a good answer."

Kincaid's own patience was recklessly thin. He'd spent the better part of the night and risked killing his palomino cow horse to get that woman out of Purgatory Canyon. Now this pipsqueak was wanting to make something else out of it.

"I'll talk when these two girlfriends of yours take this rope off," he said in an even tone.

Alamo took a half-step to one side. Before Kincaid could shift his eyes to the little man, he felt a gun-barrel-heavy jolt against his cheekbone. His knees turned suddenly watery and he sagged to the ground, tasting the saltiness of his own blood.

When he raised his head the heavy six-gun had returned to its lavishly embossed holster.

The words he heard were calm, spoken without emotion.

"You don't hear so good, cowboy. I'm gonna ask you once more. How'd she come by them wounds?"

Blondy's ears were still ringing.

"I heard you were fast with a gun, Alamo. Ever try drawing against a man who didn't have his arms tied?"

If he had spat in the short man's face, the result couldn't have been more volatile. Alamo Sam's face turned crimson. His eyes bulged against their sockets.

"I'll have your hide for that, you wise bastard." He licked his lips. "Take that rope off him."

He has guts, Blondy thought. But a minute later he understood that it wasn't a fair stand-up fight that Alamo Sam had in mind.

"Hold his arms," he commanded Red and Wilbanks.

Then the little man stood on tiptoe and glared into Kincaid's face.

"You're gonna rue the day you got smart with Alamo Sam, mister. First, though, there's a thing or two you might oughta know."

He paused and spat in the dust between Blondy's boots.

"Nobody guns a Hatchet rider and gets by without payin' for it."

There was ice in the pale eyes looking up at him. Kincaid was surprised at the emotion that charged the next words.

"And that young lady on your bunk is Mr. Detwiler's niece!"

Blondy opened his mouth to speak. At that instant Alamo Sam's fist moved with the same suddenness his gun hand had. The air left Kincaid's lungs in a rush. Involuntarily he bent over. Alamo's knee met his face squarely. He felt the blood erupt from his nose.

He heard the little man talking, but the

words were thin and faraway.

"... and the last time you'll steal a Hatchet cow!"

A fist crashed against the cheekbone where the gun barrel had struck before. Kincaid would have fallen, but the two men holding his arms jerked him upright again. Then the Hatchet ramrod began methodically to ensure that no part of his anatomy went untouched. Blow after blow ripped into his face, his rib cage, his belly. It went on, Blondy thought, for a hell of a long time.

At last he lay curled on his side in the dust. With one eye he looked on a fancy boot, the sharp toe covered with a silver cap. The boot moved quickly, and he felt it drive deep into his stomach. He retched, fighting for air, until unconsciousness closed in.

The shadows were long on the shoulders of Purgatory Mountain when he came to. He lay for a long while trying to remember what it was that had happened. Thrown and dragged by an old bronc, probably, he concluded. Then the events of the morning returned in a painful rush.

He tried to move. Pain, like coiled barbed wire, laced through every muscle and sinew in his body. He lay back, his mind doggedly pursuing a single thought: Would he ever mend sufficiently to stand and face Alamo Sam over the barrel of his Colt's?

He felt the throb of footsteps in the earth against which he lay. With the one eye which wasn't swollen shut he looked through the grass to a pair of boots standing three steps away. Involuntarily he flinched. But these weren't fancy, hand-stitched, hair-out calfskin. These were run-down, worn-out boots that were two seasons beyond their life expectancy.

"You're a tough son-of-a-buck, I'll say that. I figured you for dead."

The voice was neither hostile nor friendly. The observation was matter-of-fact, the same tone a man would use reporting the count of steers in a day's gather.

Blondy's eye moved upward to the man's face. He recognized him, the skinny, stooped cowhand with the shaggy black mustache who had announced his arrival to the Hatchet foreman. Well, they must have left a man behind to ensure that Blondy Kincaid didn't live to see sundown. At the moment, he wasn't sure he cared.

He levered himself up on one elbow, closing his good eye until the mountainside stopped spinning. When he spoke, his voice was little more than a ragged grunt.

"Where's Alamo?"

"Him and the boys rode out. Long time ago."

Blondy nodded toward the cabin.

"What about the woman?"

The other man hunkered down, careful to keep his spurs from gouging his thighs.

"They took her back to the Hatchet. Rigged one of them travois like the Injuns use."

Kincaid considered that for a time.

"Why did they leave you here?"

The stooped man spat a stream of tobacco juice into the dust and wiped his mustache with the sleeve of his shirt. He swallowed the residue, his well-defined Adam's apple registering the function.

"Well, Alamo thought maybe you hadn't got the drift of what he was tryin' to say. So I was to stick around and explain it again. If you was alive. If you wasn't, then I was going to dig you a grave."

Blondy grinned, feeling his face crack.

"Nice guy, that ramrod. What was the message he was so concerned about me getting."

"That you leave the country as quick as you're able to straddle a hoss."

Kincaid struggled to his feet and stood

there a long time, swaying like a drunken man. The Hatchet cowboy stood a few steps away and watched.

"What you got in mind?" he asked, not fear, but a hint of caution in his tone.

Blondy aimed his good eye down the slope.

"I'm going down to the spring to clean up. Soon as this mountain settles down."

It was a long, agonizing walk. Disaster loomed at every step. He fell before he reached the little trickle of water and had to crawl the final few steps. The skinny cowboy walked a step behind him, never offering a hand.

The icy water against the bruised and torn flesh of his face was like another blow from Alamo Sam's fists. But after a time Blondy began to feel life flowing back into his body. He lay back on the grass and looked up at the other man.

"What do they call you?"

"Double-ugly. And some other things. Name's Rivers, though."

"How long you been with the Hatchet?"

"Not too long a spell. Less than a year, I'd say."

"That Alamo Sam gent didn't learn his manners in Sunday school," Blondy said conversationally. "I suppose he's Slick Detwiler's fair-haired boy."

Rivers nodded, making marks in the dirt with a twig.

"Yep. There's somethin' else you maybe ought to know. That girl. Detwiler's niece. Alamo has got the sweets for her somethin' awful. He's planning on marryin' her one of these days."

Blondy grunted with new understanding.

"And getting his hands on the whole Hatchet outfit, I'd guess." He didn't wait for Rivers to agree. "I got the definite impression his nose was pretty badly out of joint about something."

He speared Rivers with a cold gaze.

"I didn't hurt the girl. Found her over in the big canyon, after her horse spooked."

The Hatchet cowboy looked embarrassed.

"Well, yeah. We found where it happened. Even found some of her hair on the limb of that tree. Alamo knew how she come to get hurt."

He paused a moment, then added in a low voice, "Alamo don't like nobody who ain't afraid to stand up to him."

Kincaid fished in his shirt pocket, drew out a half-damp sack of makings, and offered the tobacco to Rivers.

"You don't sound so all-fired happy with

him your own self."

Rivers studied the cigarette he was rolling, saying nothing. At last he licked the seam and slipped one end of the cylinder into his mouth. He lit it and looked at Kincaid through the curl of blue smoke.

"My old daddy brought me up to believe it ain't exactly fair for a gent to beat hell out of somebody while two other gents holds that somebody's arms."

But after a moment he shrugged.

"Guess it ain't none of my lookout, though, long as the Hatchet pays my wages."

The two of them sat in the patch of grass around the little spring and watched the sun disappear between the swell of the twin peaks. Kincaid wasn't sure what Alamo Sam's instructions to this neighborly sort of cowpuncher might have been, but it wouldn't hurt a thing to try to get a couple of answers.

"What's this Detwiler hombre have against the Rafter G?" he asked, keeping his voice casual. "Seems to me it's mighty poor business for a couple of cattlemen to have a war going all the time just because their ranges run side by side."

Rivers ground the cigarette stub beneath a run-over boot heel.

"They said you was new to these parts. I

can sure believe it, you askin' questions like that. This particular war goes back a long ways. It's Grimm and Detwiler fightin' now, but before that it was Grimm and some Englishman that had the Hatchet outfit for a little while. But before that it was Grimm and a highfalutin gent named Colonel Webster Buchanan.

"Every time the Hatchet changed hands, the feud with the Rafter G just went right on."

With the same casualness, Blondy asked, "What kind of jasper was this Colonel Webster Buchanan?"

Rivers' heavy black brows puckered.

"That was before my time. But from what I've been told, he was pretty taken with hisself. Thought he ought to own the whole territory. Anybody he couldn't buy out or beat out got the stuffin's stomped out of 'em."

Kincaid knew the story, but he couldn't resist asking.

"What happened to him?"

The lean puncher with the stooped shoulders shook his head.

"The way I hear it, the Colonel got his comeuppance. In spades. I guess there wasn't a soul in the territory that didn't feel sorry for him and his missus. The Colonel was already along in years when they had themselves a little girl. Cute as a filly colt, they say. Miz Webster was takin' a drive in the colonel's fancy buggy one day, down along the Piedra River. She stopped the buggy and got out for a minute, and left the baby on the seat."

He stopped.

"Well, what happened?" Blondy prodded.

"Somethin'—or somebody—spooked that old horse. He ended up in the Piedra, that buggy nothin' but mess of kindlin' wood behind him."

"And the baby?"

"Drowned. Washed down the river. They never did find the little tyke's body." He shook his head. "Weren't long after that when Buchanan sold out to the Englishman and left the country. I don't have no idea what became of him."

Kincaid let the silence drag on for a time. At last he asked, "Is it all Grimm's doing? The hard feelings between Hatchet and the Rafter G?"

"Well, now," Rivers grunted. "I'm just a workin' stiff. When the ramrod tells me to ride the boundary to make sure no Hatchet calves end up wearin' a Rafter G brand on their hip, I just do what I'm told."

"You saying Old Man Grimm is swinging a wide loop?"

The puncher shrugged.

"Like I said, I'm just a workin' stiff." He grinned. "I'd be much obliged for another round of them makin's in your shirt pocket."

Blondy bathed his swollen features in the cold spring water again and got to his feet. Every muscle screamed.

"I'm going to have to kill that Hatchet ramrod, Slim. You understand that."

"A man does what he has to do," Rivers grunted. "Anyway, after what I seen him do to you today, I sort of made up my mind to get shut of him and the whole Hatchet outfit."

Kincaid turned and started slowly up the slope.

"Let's see if we can rustle up some grub," he said.

12

The following morning Kincaid felt as though he'd been jerked through a knothole sideways, and he had only one good eye with which to see, but moving around was better than lying on the bunk. He and Rivers saddled their horses and rode down past the spring beyond the grove of aspens to the pens where Blondy had put the cattle he'd gathered.

What he saw almost made his swollen eye open. The pens had been jerked down and scattered across the meadow. There wasn't hide or hair of a cow in sight.

"Uh, I forgot to mention it," Rivers said diffidently. "Alamo wanted to be sure you understood what he said about clearin' out of the territory."

Kincaid sat for several minutes in his saddle, squinting through one eye at the devastation the Hatchet foreman had left behind.

For the moment he had forgotten that his purpose in coming to the Rafter G was to pick the bones of one Orlando Grimm. All he could think of now was the hard work he'd put in gathering that handful of elusive livestock.

"I've changed my mind," he said at last to no one in particular. "I'm not going to kill that sawed-off little bastard."

Rivers' heavy brows jerked up in surprise. "You ain't?"

"I'm going to tear his eyelids off and stake him out on an anthill. He sure does know how to make a fellow mad."

Rivers cleared his throat.

"I'd best be movin' on. Hate to have Alamo show up and find out I ain't workin' for Hatchet any longer. He takes things like that personal."

"What're you figuring on doing?" Blondy inquired.

"Take me a little holiday, I reckon. Spend some of this *dinero* I ain't had a chance to spend in four or five months."

Kincaid put out a hand.

"Good luck."

"Same to you." Rivers nodded. "No hard feelin's, amigo."

Blondy watched the spare, hump-shouldered cowboy ride away into the trees, then turned and kneed the palomino back up the slope. Inside the line shack, he gathered up his meager store of belongings, lashed his war bag to the back of the bay gelding, and swung astride the stallion again. To hell with the whole damned thing, he told himself suddenly. His fight with Alamo Sam would have to wait until some other time. The first thing he was going to do was to ride back to the Rafter G and tell Old Man Grimm what he thought of his ancestry, and then he was heading south to Mexico. Colonel Webster Buchanan and Orlando Grimm could go to the devil in double harness. They deserved each other.

He started to smile at sweet recollections of life south of the Rio Grande River, but the smile wouldn't stay put. It was only partially because the flesh of his jaws and around his eyes was still bruised and swollen. He swore aloud, drawing a quick twitch of the ears from the palomino.

"What the hell has gotten into you, Kincaid? Wasting time worrying about Old Man Grimm's daughter! Him and her are just as alike as two peas in a pod. Soured on the whole world. Always afraid somebody is going to try to beat them out of a *peso*. Why, that skinny Dru Lee kid can't tell a sure-enough cowboy from a bag of wind soaked in bay rum."

He reached up and jerked his hat down until it rested on the bridge of his swollen nose, and glared out at a narrow world of sawtooth mountaintops. But like a dogie calf tied to his saddle horn, he couldn't shake the picture of the girl: binding the ugly wound in her father's backside; cooking breakfast and looking as cool and unperturbed as though she hadn't spent all night and fifteen hundred dollars bailing him out of Sheriff Dollarhide's jail; or scalding him with angry eyes when he expressed his opinion about Garrett Haley.

He leaned forward with a forearm resting on the saddle horn and spoke his thoughts to the ears of the palomino stud.

"The hell of it is, if I was to jerk Orlando Grimm's little empire down around his ears, she'd get caught right square in the middle."

But somehow the idea of riding away to Mexico and leaving it all behind wasn't nearly as appealing as it had been an hour earlier.

The trail the palomino had been following fell suddenly away, disappearing through a cleft in the stone battlement that crowned the canyon before him. He moved to the brink of the drop-off and looked into a sheer-sided abyss that cut a wedge a thousand feet deep out of the side of the mountain. Far below through a blue haze of distance, he saw a sparkling little necklace of spring-fed water curling along the canyon floor.

But the trail down the mountainside wasn't the perilous path of light-stepping game animals that he had expected to find. Instead, it looped down the precipitous incline in a series of moderately gentle switchbacks, a route instinctively chosen by cattle bound for the canyon floor and the water supply on which they depended for survival.

Kincaid sat for a long time studying the deep, ragged gorge, his cattleman's instinct gauging the possibilities. This Purgatory Canyon range was alive with cattle that needed to be wearing the Rafter G brand. But as Shorty had aptly pointed out to Grimm, it would take a heap of cowboyin' to chouse 'em out of this country, country that God hadn't finished working on yet.

At last, satisfied with his musings, Blondy sent the two horses through the defile and down the switchback trail. A half-hour later they emerged from the trees to the grassy banks of the little stream. A handful of cows and calves abandoned the watercourse and fled into the timber. Blondy hobbled the horses, stripped them of saddle and pack, and turned them loose to graze. Then he shed his clothes and waded grudgingly into the icy water.

The bath was torture, pure and simple, but when it was over he felt like grinning for the first time since yesterday's sunrise. He could see through both eyes again, his lips were back to near-normal size, and the bullet wound in his shoulder was little more than a vague stiffness.

He dragged his gear to the edge of the timber, built a small fire for the coffeepot, and settled back against the trunk of a ponderosa to cogitate. Since coming to the Rafter G, he'd managed to kill a couple of hombres who needed killing, pick up a murder charge, make some new enemies, and develop an acre or so of bruises and aching muscles—but he was still no closer to settling Orlando Grimm's hash than the day he came.

The problem was gnawing at Blondy's innards when he crawled into his bedroll, and was still there when he awoke before sunup. He set about cooking breakfast, and as the first shafts of sunlight began to set the peaks ablaze, he took the trees around him into his confidence.

"Sure. You can ride away and forget your deal with the Colonel. Spend the rest of your days in Mexico while the law up here lays back and waits to put a noose around your neck anytime you cross the border. And you can forget Dru Lee, too. Who cares if she marries that Garrett Haley tinhorn and has a half-dozen of his kids?"

He burned his thumb on the skillet in which the salt pork was sizzling, and swore long and in great detail.

"Now that you've got all that foolishness out of your system, just get on about gathering Rafter G beef. That's what you rode up here for."

He felt better for the making of the decision, even though it solved nothing. He left his bedroll and gear under the trees, saddled the bay, and rode down the canyon. It suited his purposes better than he'd hoped. Except for the cow trail leading down the mountain, the gorge was a natural enclosure. Nothing short of an eagle could scale its sheer stone-ribbed walls.

Like a wasp's waist, the canyon pinched down to a passage no more than fifty yards wide at one point before spreading into a broader, gentler canyon downstream. It was the kind of bottleneck Blondy had hoped to find. He took down his lariat, roped the butt end of a massive fallen ponderosa pine, and dragged it into place.

For the remainder of that day and throughout the next, Kincaid rode hard and long, swapping horses often. By sundown of the second day the narrow neck of the box canyon was sealed off by a breastwork of dead timber that spanned the little stream from one rocky canyon shoulder to the other.

He shifted his saddle back to the palomino, left his bedroll and the bay gelding in the trees beside the clearing, and headed up the switchback trail the mountain cattle followed when they had to leave the sanctuary of the high-country timber to slake their thirst.

It was hardly past midmorning when he dragged the final length of dead timber into place across the trail that sliced through the rocky parapet girdling the canyon's upper rim. He sat with his knee hooked around the saddle horn while he smoked a cigarette and surveyed the results of his labors. The box canyon was now, in truth, a box. The all-but-vertical walls of the quarter-mile length of canyon were matched at both ends by barriers that no four-legged critter could surmount, no matter how badly he might want water.

It took four days for Blondy's scheme to pay off. From his camp in the depths of the canyon, he heard the lamenting begin. At first it was an occasional bellow that floated down to him on the thin mountain air, but little by little it grew, until by the third day it was an unceasing crescendo of sound. The mountains rang with the lamentation of thirsty cattle.

At sunrise on the fourth day, he lashed his gear onto the bay, saddled the palomino, and rode up the snakelike trail to the barricade that blocked its mouth. The sight that greeted him caused him to chuckle aloud. Bunched in an eddying ocean on the mountain top were several hundred cattle, driven from covert in the rugged high country by a common suffering—thirst.

Kincaid dragged the breastwork of timber from the trail and sat his horse a short distance away, watching. With tongues hanging long, bawling plaintively, they headed down the trail, cows and calves and old mossy-horned steers that hadn't let a man on a horse within rifle shot of them for years. Now they took no notice of the mounted cowboy. It was water they wanted.

When the last of the herd had crowded through the rocky defile onto the narrow trail leading to the canyon floor, Blondy once more closed the trail with a fortification of timber. Those several hundred head of wild mountain cattle would remain imprisoned in his box canyon for as long as he wanted them there.

13

A day and a half later, he rode into the headquarters of the Rafter G. In the shank of the afternoon, Shorty and Chorizo and McHenry were turning their horses into the corral. To his surprise, Garrett Haley was there also, unsaddling a horse that showed signs of hard riding.

Shorty looked him over silently for a moment, then spat tobacco juice into the dust.

"What in blazes happened to yore face? Get kicked by a horse?"

The bruises were well along toward healing, but the memory of Alamo Sam was still a raw wound in Kincaid's mind.

"Your friends over at Hatchet paid me a visit," he said evenly.

"I told you to steer clear of them coyotes. You can't gather cattle and fight a war at the same time." The bewhiskered foreman paused and dropped his head, looking up at

Blondy through the gray tangle of his bushy eyebrows. "I s'pose you're going to tell us that Alamo Sam and his boys whipped you to a standstill and then run off all the stock you'd gathered."

He grinned a knowing grin and turned to McHenry.

"All right. That's ten you owe me. I told you he'd come back with his tail between his legs, and nary a cow penned up."

Blondy stopped in the middle of unsaddling and eyed the bowlegged ramrod.

"You mean to tell me you expected them Hatchet hombres to show up while I was up on the Purgatory? I thought you tole me everything this side of the peaks was Rafter G country."

Shorty's grin disappeared.

"What I told you was right. But Detwiler and that ornery ramrod of his get careless about boundaries sometimes. Think they own the whole damn territory."

Kincaid leveled a hard gaze at the foreman.

"While he was having his fun kicking my insides out, Alamo Sam said something about the Rafter G stealing Hatchet livestock. You wouldn't have any idea what he was talking about, I suppose."

But there was no answer from Shorty. He

had disappeared into the shed with his saddle.

Trailing behind Haley, they trooped to the washstand outside the back door. Cleaned up and with the dust beaten from their clothes, they went on into the rambling ranch house. In the kitchen, Dru Lee turned from the stove and saw Kincaid. Her eyes went wide.

Leaning on his cane, Grimm hobbled in.

"What in tarnation got aholt of you, boy?"

"Alamo Sam," said Blondy.

Grimm scowled blackly.

"I suppose that means you didn't get no stock gathered. Hell fire, we'll be all winter gettin' 'em out of that Purgatory country."

"I got a few head penned up," Kincaid said.

Shorty looked up from his plate.

"I thought you said you didn't do no good."

"I didn't say that. You did."

"How many?" Grimm interrupted.

"Four hundred seventeen head."

Shorty coughed, strangling on a mouthful of steak. Finally he said, "There ain't no way you could've rounded up four hundred head of them wild critters up on the Purgatory. For one thing, them pens won't hold near that many."

Blondy let the silence drag on for a full minute while he gave attention to his plate.

"Alamo Sam and his crew tore down the pens."

Shorty started to swear, then glanced up at Dru Lee and stopped.

"I suppose you got all four hundred of them critters tied to a tree?"

The sarcasm lay heavy behind his words.

Blondy fixed the aging puncher with a steady gaze.

"It's not so hard. If a fellow has more brains than a cow. I let 'em get a little thirsty, then trapped 'em in a box canyon."

Orlando Grimm broke into a laugh.

"Shorty, you might be smart to ask this young feller for some advice about gatherin' beef. He's done damn nigh as much as you four so-called cowhands put together."

Shorty was scowling at his plate, his face crimson. It was Garrett Haley who broke the silence.

"A man ought to learn to take care of himself with his fists in this country. Either that or go on back to where he came from."

It was said casually, without fervor. But the conversation around the table came to an abrupt halt.

Kincaid looked across at Haley. His voice

was almost pleasant.

"The first thing a man ought to do is learn to keep his mouth shut. If he don't, somebody's sure liable to give him a lesson in manners."

The color was rising in Garrett Haley's cheeks.

"If there's any teaching to be done, I'll do it," he snapped. "No smart-mouth son—"

"Garrett!" Dru Lee's voice was pitched high with emotion. "Would you like some pie? I found some wild plums along the creek bed. Not many are ripe yet, but enough to make a pie."

Grimm had sat with a half-smile on his face while he listened to the exchange between Kincaid and Haley. But his daughter's concern stirred him to take a hand.

"You boys settle down. Save that vinegar for roundin' up cattle." He pointed at Kincaid's breastbone with his fork. "Tell me about this run-in you had with Alamo Sam and his Hatchet boys. What'd you do to set 'em off?"

"They came to the line shack looking for the girl."

Six pairs of eyes swung round toward Blondy. Dru Lee forgot she was pouring coffee into Garrett Haley's cup. The brown liquid spilled over, spreading in a circle on the oilcloth.

"What girl?" Shorty breathed.

"Detwiler's niece, I think they said." Blondy was very much aware of Dru Lee's eyes on him. What he said next was for her benefit. "A real good-lookin' woman, too. Long black hair. A fine figure. And sure doesn't talk a man to death."

Grimm's scowl had grown still deeper.

"Sounds to me like you were askin' for trouble. I told you there ain't going to be no feudin' with the Hatchet until roundup is over and done with. After that you can do anything you damn well please."

McHenry had sat silently through the heated talk. Now he spoke.

"I ain't afflicted with politeness like these other folks. What in tarnation was Slick Detwiler's niece doing at the line shack with you?"

Instantly Dru Lee was on her feet, moving away to a distant corner of the room, as though she wanted to be too far away to hear. But Blondy didn't get a chance to answer.

"You're not too bright, McHenry," Garrett Haley said. "There's only one reason a grown man would have himself a woman hid away at a shack in the hills."

He turned and looked hard at Grimm.

"What I can't figure is, why would any outfit keep such a man on the payroll? He ought to be horsewhipped and run off like a chicken-killin' hound."

Kincaid's voice was low and easy.

"Problem is, there's nobody around here man enough to do that, Haley."

Orlando Grimm's fist came down hard on the table edge. Plates and dishes rattled.

"I'm still runnin' this lash-up. And I told you boys there ain't going to be no private feuds while there's still cattle to be gathered. Not until every four-legged critter on Rafter G range is brought in, branded, and ready to trail out."

Kincaid turned away from Haley's smoldering countenance.

"Maybe I didn't hear you right, Grimm. Any cowman with a lick of sense knows you don't sell off your mother cows if you figure on staying in business another year."

Grimm's face took on a smug look, but instead of answering, he went on eating. It was Shorty who spoke.

"There's cowmen, and there's cowmen, Kincaid. The boss here is just a shade smarter than most. Why, he's figured out—"

Grimm suddenly slashed the air over the

table with his knife, cutting off the foreman's words. If there was to be any more said on the subject, he was going to do the saying.

"I suppose it won't hurt none to tell it, but I don't want this goin' beyond these here walls." He chewed meditatively for a moment, then wiped his mouth with his sleeve. "I've been runnin' cows in the territory since before you was borned, Kincaid. Through good times and some damn bad ones. Well, the last three or four years have been pretty good years for the cow business. Every shade-tree outfit from the Brazos River to the Rocky Mountains has been trailin' north with anything that wore hair and carried a pound of beef."

He paused, shifting his wounded hip on the chair. Whatever he was going to say next was a profound pronouncement. He wanted to be certain his audience was paying attention.

"Well, now. The signs are all there, but there ain't one cowman in a thousand smart enough to read 'em. Too damn greedy, that's what they are." He jammed a thumb against his chest. "But this old cowboy has got it all figured out. The bottom is fixin' to fall out of the cow market just like it did in seventy-three. You mark my words. By next year you won't be able to give away a yearlin' in Chicago, much less sell one. There's going to be a passel of cowmen go bust when it happens."

He drew his pipe from a vest pocket, struck a match on the coils of the snake engraved across the big silver buckle at his midsection, and pulled at the pipe for a long moment while he studied Kincaid's face above the flame.

"That's why I want every piece of beef on the Rafter G brought in and made ready to trail north."

Kincaid grunted skeptically.

"You're taking one hell of a chance, selling off everything, including your breeding stuff."

"You're just like the rest of them, boy. Cain't see the forest for the trees. Well, the range is overstocked to hell and gone. The drought ain't left enough grass to keep a jackrabbit alive. Next year every rancher in the territory will be having to unload his herd at whatever price he can beg."

Gingerly he leaned back in his chair and hooked his thumbs beneath his suspenders.

"Yessirree, Bob! This is going to be Orlando Grimm's year."

Shorty was hunched forward until his shirtfront dragged in the beans on his plate. His tone was gleeful.

"When the dust settles, the Rafter G is gonna own just about every spread between the Rio Grande and the Pecos. Including Slick Detwiler's outfit. Ain't that a fact, boss?"

Grimm scowled at his foreman. He had disclosed all the secrets he cared to disclose. He gave Shorty a look that told him to shut his mouth, then turned back to Kincaid.

"Never mind about that. But now you savvy why I'm in such a lather to get 'em all gathered and branded."

Blondy nodded.

"Yeah, maybe so. But what I don't see is how you figure to get all this done with only five cowhands. And the Hatchet crew dropping in every few days to wreck your pens."

Grimm continued to fork beans and beef into his mouth, but his face turned thoughtful.

"You're right there, boy. I've been giving it some thought. I can't sit a saddle yet, but there is another cowhand on the place. A half-dozen ought to be enough to get the job done."

Blondy glanced around the table, his eyes registering the faces of Shorty, Chorizo, McHenry, and Garrett Haley.

"Unless my arithmetic has gone cockeyed, there's only five punchers," he said.

"That other puncher is pourin' your coffee," Grimm said, the words turning into a bray of laughter.

Kincaid didn't really mean to make it sound derisive, but the words were out of his mouth before he could stop them.

"You've got to be kidding. Poppin' the brush through those mountains after a crazy-mean longhorn isn't exactly the same sort of pastime as washing dishes or darning socks. You're not talking sense."

He felt Dru Lee's eyes burning into the back of his head. Her cheeks flamed.

"I've been riding about as long as you have, Mr. Kincaid." Her words were flint against steel. "And I've never had to beg a ride back to the ranch on somebody else's horse. Or been shot out of the saddle. Or been beaten to a pulp because I didn't know enough to mind my own business."

She stormed from the room with the curls of her short brown hair snapping against the back of her neck.

By the light of an early moon, Kincaid walked with McHenry and the Mexican to the bunkhouse. Shorty and Haley trailed behind, talking, and drifted on toward the barn. Blondy had hardly unbuckled his gunbelt and hung it on the post of his bunk when he heard the voices rising in angry stabbing words. He strolled to the door and leaned against the facing. He could see the little ramrod, his bowlegs braced wide, glaring up at Garrett Haley's face. The words floated sharp and clear through the night air.

"You'll play hell ridin' off again. I'm foreman of this here outfit, and I say we need every hand we can get on roundup. That includes you."

Towering over Shorty, Haley pushed his hat to the back of his head. Moon-etched shadows lent a wolfish snarl to his features.

"You sawed-off little runt. You're not telling me what I can do and what I can't. I'm not through with that job yet, and I plan to finish it. Roundup or no roundup."

Shorty drew himself up until his eyes were on a level with Haley's chin.

"We'll by damn see about it," he yelled. "Grimm won't stand still for you not pitchin' in with the gather. You wait and see."

Shorty turned on a heel and started away, but Haley reached out and with a big hand caught his shoulder. He jerked the smaller man about, grabbed a handful of his shirtfront with both hands, and lifted him until his feet cleared the ground.

"Don't threaten me, hear! You're not going

to tell the old man a damned thing."

He relaxed his grip, and Shorty started to drop back to the ground. But in an almost casual gesture, Haley's huge hand came around in a short backhanded arc. The blow sent the slight ramrod flying backward against the wall of the barn.

"Well, I thought you were nothing but hot air, but I can see you're plenty tough."

Blondy's words were easy, almost soft. He was standing a pace behind Haley when he said it.

Haley spun around, rage drawing his handsome features into a grimace.

"This is none of your business, cowboy. You'd best head on back to the bunkhouse unless you think you need some more of them bruises."

Blondy leaned a shoulder against the wall of the barn and looked down at the foreman, slowly gathering his feet under him.

"Shorty," said Kincaid. "What do you say we dehorn this big hombre? Sort of remind him he's not the only bull in the herd."

Garrett Haley read the signs. He had twenty pounds and a couple of inches on this lean, cocky cowboy, and he was reasonably sure he could take his measure. It was something he'd been wanting to do.

He swung while Kincaid was turned half away, and his fist collided with Kincaid's head just above the ear. Stars burst in Blondy's mind. He sagged to one knee, grabbing at the wall of the barn for support. The next instant, Haley hooked a blow at his rib cage.

Shorty had decided against getting to his feet. He'd just as soon watch this little show from a comfortable seat on the ground, he concluded. He didn't like the way the show had started, though.

Blondy took a step backward, and Haley thought it was all over. He was grinning as he moved in. He swung a roundhouse punch, a blow with enough force to tear a man's head off. He was still swinging when all the air left his lungs in a rush. Suddenly he felt the same sickness he had felt the time his one-eyed mule kicked him in the belly while being hitched to a wagon. Two more blows just like the first, and as quick as a succession of lightning bolts, buried themselves in his midsection. The roundhouse punch he had thrown faded into a limp memory.

Garrett Haley was retching for air, the painful sucking sound of a wind-broken horse, when Kincaid hit him again. The knuckles of his left fist slammed into Haley's cheekbone with a shock that Blondy felt to his shoulder. The short right jab to Haley's nose that followed was unnecessary. The big man dropped to his hands and knees and sagged there, still making unpleasant noises.

Shorty leaned over, picked up Haley's black hat from the corral dust, and jammed it backward onto the stunned cowboy's head.

"When you get to where you're going, send me a letter," he said. "I'll see you get whatever pay's coming to you."

Shorty and Kincaid sat with their backs resting against the wall of the barn and watched Garrett Haley ride slowly away in the moonlight. After a time Shorty drew out a plug of tobacco and bit off a chew.

"Weren't no need for you to put in your oar," he said to Blondy. "I'd-a had him hollerin' uncle in another minute."

"Yeah," Blondy grunted.

Shorty got to his feet.

"Well, guess I'd best go break the news to Grimm. He'll cuss and r'ar, but he won't mind. He had about the same opinion of Haley as I did."

He started away, then stopped and turned back.

"You're welcome to tell Dru Lee her boyfriend's decided to pull up stakes."

"No, thanks," said Kincaid.

14

From Dru Lee's demeanor the following morning at breakfast, Kincaid was reasonably certain Grimm had told her about Garrett Haley's sudden departure from the Rafter G. But the angry fireworks he had expected to see failed to materialize. Either she had decided to accept the inevitable, or her affection for the blustering cowboy had not been as deeply rooted as he had supposed. It lightened his spirits.

   The five of them rode out at daylight, leaving Orlando Grimm on the porch leaning on his cholla cactus cane and staring after them wistfully. Dru Lee was mounted on a pretty chestnut mare with four stocking legs and a flaxen mane. She sat the saddle as though she'd been born to it, and Blondy found his eyes wandering to her time and again. He'd ridden for many an outfit, ever since he had run away from home to make his first trail drive, and he'd punched cows alongside some mighty strange cowboys.

But he'd never ridden out on a gather with a woman along.

Watching her slender figure swaying easily on the chestnut as she rode beside Shorty, Kincaid grumbled to himself. It was Orlando Grimm's stingy nature that had brought it about. If the cussed old tightwad would pay enough wages, he could hire some more hands, even if the Rafter G was somewhat less popular than a polecat at a box supper.

Ah, though. Perhaps Grimm had provided him with the key to accomplishing his real mission at the Rafter G, the mission on which he rode for a bitter old man named Webster Buchanan. Yeah, Blondy nodded. This was the year that Grimm was going to make his big killing. He had borrowed to the limit and overstocked his range to the hilt, figuring on selling every head of livestock he owned just before the bottom fell out of the market. But Grimm's plans all depended on timing. That was the weak link.

The holding pasture was a sea of bawling cattle. Shorty pulled up and turned in his saddle.

"We'll ride the breaks out for another two,

maybe three days. Then we'll bring down Kincaid's bunch and start brandin'."

His eyes shifted to Blondy.

"We ain't looking' for trouble with Hatchet. You just remember that, and stay clear of them Lame Horse Bluffs. Savvy?"

Kincaid gazed into the seamed face, giving no sign that he'd heard.

It was a good day for the gather, the one day in a hundred when cows and calves and even savage old steers seemed to lose their wary, suspicious nature and allow themselves to be driven docilely to the trap. The sun was disappearing in the west when they penned the last bunch and headed toward the ranch house.

"By heck, it just might be that we'll have these critters on the trail ahead of the boss's calculations." Shorty grinned.

It had been gnawing at Blondy's mind all day, ever since the foreman's admonition that morning.

"It seems like a hell of a way to run an outfit to me." he grunted.

Shorty's grin faded. His head swiveled around.

"What's that supposed to mean?"

"It means if the Rafter G runs all the way to Lame Horse Bluffs, then I figure we ought to work that part of the country, too. Hatchet or no Hatchet."

He knew it was a touchy subject with the ramrod, and Shorty didn't disappoint him.

"You ain't runnin' this here spread, young feller. When I say we stay clear of the bluffs, that's the way it's going to be. I don't want to hear no more palaverin' about it."

They unsaddled and headed for the house to eat. Blondy drew McHenry aside.

"If they ask where I am, tell 'em I had a gut ache."

McHenry's eyebrows lifted, but he nodded and went on. Kincaid headed toward the bunkhouse but made a last-second detour to the smokehouse where the beef was hanging. He sliced off several pounds of meat, wrapped it in a gunnysack and returned to the horse corral.

The palomino stallion had had a day's rest and was feeling frisky. Kincaid saddled him quickly, then caught up a big Roman-nosed blue-roan horse and threw a lead rope around his neck. The job he had in mind would require plenty of traveling.

Daylight was gone and the moon hadn't yet made its appearance. Only the stars afforded light, but Blondy knew the trail to the river canyon well enough. He made a wide circle around the ranch house and set out in a long lope toward the Piedra. He wanted to be back by sunup, but it was strictly a guess whether he could make it. He was headed for a place he'd never seen.

With the blue roan trailing on the lead rope, he sent the palomino down the narrow, twisting cow trail to the bottom of the canyon, where the Piedra River filled the night with its rushing, mighty song.

Along a trail that was barely discernible in the flat of the canyon bottom, Blondy kept the two horses in a lope. It was risky business, a good way to break a horse's leg. But he'd made up his mind to it.

When the moon at last peeked reluctantly down into the canyon, Blondy breathed easier and pushed the horses to a faster pace. When the massive palisades of Lame Horse Bluffs rose out of the semidarkness above the river canyon, he pulled the horses to a halt, stripped the saddle from the heaving sides of the stallion, and pulled it tight on the roan's back. It was the work of less than three or four minutes, and he slid into the saddle on the Roman-nosed blue horse.

The roan humped his back, his instincts urging him to unload the weight astride his spine, but the hurried miles they already had traveled drained his resolve. On they went, moving now into country totally unfamiliar to Kincaid. He was beginning to wish he'd pressed Shorty for more details about the layout of the Hatchet headquarters.

As he pushed on, Blondy began to have his doubts. Had he somehow missed the ranch headquarters altogether? If that were the case, Blondy Kincaid would have one hell of a long ride for nothing. He was giving serious thought to turning back when he heard a sound that gladdened his heart—the mournful bay of a dog, somewhere up ahead and a few points to the left of the big canyon's course.

He found the trail leading from the river to the plateau above without difficulty. It was steep, but wide, a well-traveled trail. A trail for Hatchet riders.

The next few minutes would decide the success or failure of this foolhardy mission, Kincaid knew. And failure would be fatally unpleasant.

From a saddlebag he withdrew the huge mound of meat he had carved from the side of beef hanging in Orlando Grimm's smokehouse and moved up the trail cautiously. He heard a dog bark again, a silence that lasted a minute, and then an ominous muttering in anxious canine throats. The moon showed him a pair of dogs, huge brutes, racing down the trail toward him. Beyond them, on a ridge a quarter-mile away, he could make out a collection of buildings. If the dogs continued to bark, it would be only a matter of minutes before lights began to show and humans began to stir among those buildings.

He threw a large piece of the meat toward the onrushing dogs. It was as he had hoped. They weren't a pampered, well-fed kind of settlement dog; they were hunting hounds, left to feed or starve as their instincts drove them. They quarreled momentarily over the choice find, tore the meat apart, and wolfed it down. Blondy was ready with more, but he made them come to him to get it.

In minutes the fearsome hounds were wagging their tails, pleading for another handout of red meat. Kincaid obliged, gave them each a quick chance to sniff at his hand, and resumed his stealthy approach to the headquarters of Slick Detwiler's Hatchet Ranch.

Catching sight of the bunkhouse, situated a little beyond the aging native-stone mansion that Colonel Buchanan must have built a quarter-century in the past, Kincaid momentarily checked his mounts. Somewhere among those dwellings was a man named Alamo Sam, a man with whom he had high accounts to settle.

Finally he shook his head.

"Huh-uh. Not yet, Alamo," he muttered.

Blondy swung the horses from the trail and made a wide detour around the buildings. A hundred yards beyond were the horse corrals.

A half-dozen horses were in a small pen, the remaining hundred or more in a larger pasture that extended into the darkness toward the upward sweep of mountains encircling the ranch headquarters.

It took Blondy less than five minutes to execute his scheme. He swung open the gate to the corral, then opened the pasture gate and rode in. At first the horses were hesitant, apprehensive of the night rider. But when the first one found the opening, the others followed quickly. All but one. An albino-looking cow pony that turned just before he reached the gate and floated away in the darkness. Blondy swore at him and let him go.

The herd thundered out of the corral and headed directly toward the houses, Kincaid shouting at the top of his voice and riding close on their heels. The dogs joined the cavalcade, barking wildly at the stampeding animals.

The bolting horses swept down through the

buildings and on toward the river canyon, a roiling silver cloud of dust closing in behind them. Belatedly a lamp appeared in a second-floor window of the big house. Blondy turned and saw the bunkhouse door swing open and a half-naked figure hurry out. The sound of cursing faded behind him as he rode the rumps of the stragglers toward the steep trail ahead.

The racing herd plunged down the incline toward the winding slash of silver far below. Blondy laughed into the wind. The Hatchet crew was going to be afoot for a long time.

They reached the bottom of the canyon in a stampede of flying stones, trampled brush, and a whirlwind of dust. There the herd split, some turning upstream, some down, and a sizable number plunging into the swift current of the Piedra, bound for limitless freedom on the far bank.

A good night's work, Kincaid grunted. Unfortunately, the night wasn't over.

He shifted the saddle back to the stallion, stepped astride the big horse, and set out on the long trail toward home, while the moon swam down toward the peaks behind him.

There was a hint of grayness along the eastern horizon when he rode onto the rise above the Rafter G headquarters. Dru Lee was up, starting breakfast as though the twelve hard hours of riding the day before meant nothing. Orlando Grimm might be a miserly old pirate, but his daughter was a thoroughbred, from forelock to fetlock.

Blondy had unsaddled and washed up by the time the meal was ready. As they seated themselves around the table, Shorty looked across at Kincaid and scowled.

"Couldn't sleep, huh?"

Blondy nodded.

"Nary a wink. Must have been something I ate."

Shorty's attention was fixed on his plate, but he muttered, "Yeah, sure. More likely went into town for some carousin'."

Grimm limped out to the corrals and leaned against a gatepost while the five riders saddled their horses. They had mounted up and were ready to move out when he spoke.

"Time's growin' short. I can feel a change in the weather already. I don't want nobody slackin' off, hear?" He stopped, seeming suddenly to remember his daughter was among the cowhands he was admonishing. "Now, Dru. You let them ride the rough country. Come on in early if you get worn out."

She didn't want special concessions, Blondy saw. Reining her horse away from Grimm, she said over her shoulder, "Don't worry about me."

As they filed out of the gate, Grimm's cane stabbed the air like the staff of a guidon. He shouted so there would be no mistaking his words.

"One more thing. I don't want nobody ridin' the bluffs. Just leave them be. Hear? I don't want to give Detwiler's bunch any reason to throw any lead."

Don't worry, Blondy said under his breath. *Those Hatchet cowboys have got other things on their minds today.*

At the lip of the river canyon they drew rein. In terse phrases, Shorty gave his orders. He didn't mention Lame Horse Bluffs, but before he turned away, he glared at Kincaid.

"Let's see if you can put in one good day's work without stirrin' up a hornet's nest."

Kincaid stepped down and began to tighten the cinch on the blood bay horse he was riding, while the others fanned out and disappeared into the network of ridges and ravines that scarred the plateau above the river. When he was back in the saddle, he spurred the bay into a long lope westward in the direction of Lame Horse Bluffs.

A rising wind whipped against his face. He saw, lying low against the western horizon, a bank of clouds, solid clouds heavy with moisture. Grimm was right. A change in the weather was in the making.

Kincaid drew rein on a point above the little valley that nestled against the base of Lame Horse Bluffs and marveled again at what he saw: a natural retreat for cattle, grasses flourishing beneath a jungle of squat trees and brush.

"Grimm's a fool, Or worse. Even a fool would have sense enough to know there's livestock aplenty in here," he told the bay horse.

He rode into the tangle of brush and trees and cactus and rode out again late in the afternoon, a mass of cuts and tears and punctures despite his bull-hide chaps. He had rounded up half-a-hundred head of livestock, a good day's gather.

Dru Lee, McHenry, and Chorizo were sitting their horses at the gate to the pasture. Shorty was nowhere in sight, a circumstance that suited Kincaid. The foreman might wonder how a single rider had managed to collect that sizable a bunch.

Chorizo noticed, though, and grinned broadly, his head bobbing up and down.

McHenry made a quick count as he closed the gate behind the last calf.

"A tolerable good day's gather, I'd say." He squinted appraisingly at Kincaid. "If you was to tell the rest of us pore dumb cowpokes how you managed to gather up that many critters in one day, we could finish this job in short order and go have us a holiday in town. I hear there's some whiskey in Arrowhead that ain't been drunk."

"Hard work, amigo." Blondy grinned. "That's the secret."

Dru Lee's voice was neither friendly nor otherwise.

"I thought Shorty wanted you to ride out the river canyon today. But you came from the direction of the bluffs."

It irritated Kincaid. She was too close to the truth.

"Well, now. If you think that bunch of critters came from behind the wrong rock, we'll just turn the rascals loose. Can't have 'em influencing the whole herd."

She flushed at the sarcasm in his voice, started to speak again, but instead jerked her horse around. Without a backward look she sent the pony in a run toward the ranch house.

McHenry spat a brown stream into the dust and wiped at his chin with the heel of his hand.

"Ain't any of my lookout, but it appears to me you were a bit hard on the little gal, Kincaid."

Blondy's eyes held a hint of warning.

"You're one hundred percent correct, amigo. It's none of your business."

But McHenry wasn't through. Either he failed to see the ominous light in Kincaid's eyes or he chose to ignore it.

"When it comes to roundin' up cattle or handlin' a six-gun, you're plenty handy, Kincaid. Too bad your brain turns to cow manure when it comes to dealin' with women."

Blondy reached across and caught a handful of McHenry's shirt sleeve.

"Care to explain what the hell that means before I rearrange your face?"

McHenry wasn't intimidated. He calmly returned Blondy's gaze.

"If your disposition wasn't so all-fired sour, you might make friends with that pretty little cowpuncher."

Kincaid released the other man's shirt.

"You've got a big mouth, Mac. In the first place, she's about as fond of me as a boil on the back of her neck. And in the second place, I don't give a hoot. Now, why don't you keep your bright ideas to yourself?"

McHenry shrugged.

"Try to do a man a favor, and what do you get?" He paused, watching Shorty push a handful of cows and calves down the slope toward the gate. "She was right, too, Kincaid. About where you gathered up those critters you brought in."

Kincaid started to fire an angry salvo at the other man, but stopped suddenly.

"Tomorrow you ride with me. I've got something to show you. And keep your trap shut about it."

15

They awoke the following morning to cold, drizzly skies. Grimm's prediction had come true. As the five riders fanned out away from the ranch headquarters, the old man stood on the front step and shook his cane in the air.

"You ain't got much time to get it done, hear?"

They could hear him cursing the wound in his buttocks as the house faded from sight below the ridge.

With McHenry trailing behind him, Kincaid sent the palomino stallion down the steep trail into the Piedra River gorge. No sense in letting Shorty know what he was up to, Blondy had decided. Cutting straight across the plateau to Lame Horse Bluffs would have saved a considerable amount of time, but he wasn't yet ready to announce what he'd found in the narrow valley beneath the towering limestone palisade.

McHenry gigged his horse alongside the palomino and shouted above the roar of the river.

"What is it you was so anxious to show me, Kincaid? I ain't all that taken with the scenery down here in the bottom of this ol' canyon."

Blondy gave him a go-to-hell look and loped on ahead. Suddenly, eerily, Lame Horse Bluffs appeared out of the mist above them. It was time to climb out of the canyon to the plateau above. Kincaid spurred up the steep side of the gorge, the palomino fighting for a foothold in the rocks and shale. He could hear McHenry behind him, telling his horse that the man they were following had undoubtedly taken leave of his senses.

They topped out forty-five minutes later and drew rein at the rim of the basin that swept away like a gray-green surf to the base of the bluffs. The fine, chill drizzle was beginning to turn to rain. Both men untied their slickers and pulled them on while their winded horses rested after the steep climb.

McHenry rolled a cigarette and tried unsuccessfully to light the damp cylinder. At last he gave up, threw it aside, and drew a ragged plug of tobacco from his shirt pocket.

"I don't like to seem ungrateful, pardner,"

he said. "But is this what we come all that distance to admire?"

"Keep your shirt on," Blondy said, and sent his horse down the brief, steep slope to the floor of the valley.

It was not a pleasant excursion. The tight fabric of trees and brush stubbornly resisted their movement. Every juniper under which they rode spilled a cold shower of rain down their necks. Branches whipped across their chilled faces. Long fingers of cholla cactus drove their barbed spines into the horses' legs and even through their heavy chaps.

In a small clearing hardly large enough for the two horses to stand side by side, Kincaid reined up. Some distance ahead, the raw limestone parapet called Lame Horse Bluffs, looking for all the world like the wall of a medieval castle, shot upward to disappear in the low-hanging clouds.

"This is a hell of a lot of fun," McHenry said wryly. "But I've had about all of it I care to enjoy in one dose. What do ya say we get our backsides out of this gosh-awful thicket?"

"No, not yet." Blondy shook his head. "I want to give you a look at what I saw. More danged livestock than you can shake a stick at."

"Well, I haven't seen hide nor hair of anything that resembled a cow," McHenry grumbled.

"This cold rain has probably pushed 'em over against the bluffs. Let's go."

He was right. When they came at last to the fringe of the thicket, where it washed up against the rocks at the base of the bluffs, cows and calves suddenly started appearing among the trees. A rising wind that curled down from the serrated ridge high above had merged with the chill rain to force the animals to seek shelter. They had found it in the lee of the stone fortress.

"Look at 'em!" McHenry exclaimed. "There must be hundreds of those critters in this brush. Where in blazes did they come from?"

Kincaid shook his head. "Beats me. But it's pretty obvious why they don't have any great urge to leave. Plenty of grass and water, and all kinds of cover to lay up under."

"Yeah. That's easy to figure," McHenry said. "But answer me this. Why would Old Man Grimm keep orderin' us to stay clear of this here little valley? There's as many head of livestock in this infernal patch of brush as we've gathered in a week of hard ridin' out on the open range."

Blondy watched the movement of wary

cattle in the trees around them. Finally he said, "Too many, I'd say. Something smells fishy."

"While you're workin' on solvin' this here mystery, I'm gonna build a fire and thaw out," said McHenry.

He dismounted, tied his horse to a juniper limb, and moved to the base of the bluff. The upthrust mountain of stone leaned outward from its base, forming a pocket which the rain couldn't reach. In minutes the cowboy had a small fire burning.

"I'd let a man share my fire if he was to promise to talk about women and whiskey instead of workin'," he said.

Blondy tied the palomino a few steps from McHenry's horse and came in to hunker down beside the fire.

"I think I've got it figured out," he muttered.

McHenry looked up expectantly.

"Yeah? How's that?"

"The old man has gone off his rocker. He's crazy."

But Kincaid was remembering the sharp words that had been hurled at him before: once in the saloon in Arrowhead by a man he had had to kill, and again high in the Purgatory Peaks by a man who needed killing. A man named Alamo Sam. Rustling, they had called it.

His eyes were on the mass of rain-drenched trees and brush through which he and McHenry had ridden. Deep within his mind a warning sounded. There was movement out there, movement of something that wasn't a cow or a calf. He'd had a momentary glimpse of a rider's low-pulled hat brim. Someone had followed their tracks through the underbrush.

"We've got company, Mac," he said quietly, and moved quickly away from the fire. McHenry faded several feet away in the opposite direction.

Blondy could make out the forelegs of a horse through the brush. It stopped when the rider caught sight of the other two horses. Well, he thought, he and McHenry were smack against the Hatchet boundary. If this was a jasper looking to complain, he'd find them ready.

Hunkered down beneath the outthrust shelf of limestone, Kincaid drew his Colt and waited.

The rain was building in intensity, a curtain of gray walling them off from the rest of the world. He squinted through the dimness and saw the horseman dismount. If there were others spread out through the thicket, he and McHenry were sitting ducks.

He was scanning the trees to either side when he heard McHenry's easy words.

"I wouldn't shoot, amigo."

Then he could make out the slight figure coming toward them through the mist. It was Dru Lee, her hat pulled low over her eyes and the tail of a slicker several sizes too large dragging in the mud behind her.

She looked first at McHenry, then at Kincaid, and moved in close to the fire. For several minutes no one spoke.

It was Blondy who finally broke the silence.

"What in blue blazes are you doing here?"

She was trying to keep her teeth from chattering. After a moment she said, "Following your tracks."

She pulled off her big-brimmed hat and shook the water from it. Blondy saw where the dampened ends of her brown hair were plastered to her neck.

"Why?" he asked.

She looked at him levelly, her eyes unwavering.

"Because Dad and Shorty both said no one was to work the bluffs."

Suddenly Kincaid wanted very badly to

take a poke at someone, a someone who knew the answer but wouldn't talk. He wished it were Grimm or his cantankerous ramrod standing in front of him. He'd get some answers.

Instead, he made himself take a deep breath before he spoke.

"There are hundreds of head of livestock in this thicket. I mean hundreds of 'em. Can you give me one good reason why they shouldn't be wearing a Rafter G on their hip?"

"I haven't seen any stock in here."

"Don't play games," Kincaid said. "Are you trying to tell me these aren't Rafter G animals?"

She frowned.

"I suppose any cows here would be Dad's. Everything this side of the bluffs is Rafter G."

"Well, then. Why in the dickens wouldn't they be gathered along with everything else?"

Dru Lee looked at him for a long moment. Finally her eyes wavered and she looked into the fire.

McHenry, a few steps away, spat into the flames and hitched up his cartridge belt.

"While you folks are socializin', I'm going to fetch me a flask out of that saddlebag yonder and have me a little nip agin' the chill."

He moved out from beneath the overhanging ledge of limestone toward his horse, tied to a juniper a dozen paces away. The rain had slackened markedly, and they both had their eyes on him, neither ready to concede the argument.

McHenry was in the act of unbuckling a saddlebag strap when they saw him lurch crazily against his horse. A half-second later the sound of the shot, caught and muffled by the damp, heavy air, reached their ears. On his knees, McHenry clung to a stirrup, fighting to stay erect. His horse shied away, and he fell facedown in the mud.

Dru Lee caught her breath, a tiny shriek escaping around the knuckles of the fist pressed against her lips. The sound of the shot was still hovering about them when Kincaid's Colt appeared in his hand. For the interval of a deep breath they stood that way, while the toes of McHenry's boots pushed up little trenches in the rich black mud.

Dru Lee's voice was hardly louder than a whisper. The sternness it had held a few moments earlier had vanished.

"He's still . . . still alive, isn't he?"

"I don't know. Maybe. But I've got to get him back under this ledge."

Abruptly he understood the trap they had set for themselves. A rifleman perched on the stone parapet far above them could see every move they made unless they stayed tight against the base of the cliff. The bushwhacker had done just that, waiting until one of them moved out into the open. The rain had slackened at precisely the right moment for him to draw a bead on McHenry.

"He's still moving. He's still alive." Dru Lee's hand went involuntarily to Blondy's arm.

"Yeah."

He holstered his Colt, wishing now for more rain, enough to block them from the eyes of the man above.

To Dru Lee he said, "Build up that fire. He'll need to be kept warm."

"There's no wood," she murmured, shaking her head.

"Those cow chips there. They're dry." Irritation was growing in Kincaid. It wasn't McHenry's doing. He was an innocent bystander. He, Blondy Kincaid, had insisted that the good-natured cowboy come along.

Maybe the rifleman had gone. Maybe the one shot was all he wanted. Feeling naked and vulnerable, Blondy stepped out from beneath the stone overhang, measuring the steps to the fallen cowboy.

He was halfway there when the sudden lethal slap of a slug hitting the mud sounded a foot from him. Before the booming thunder of the shot reached his ears, he had thrown himself back under the ledge. He crouched there on hands and knees, breathing hard and watching the man sprawled in the mud an eternal dozen paces away.

McHenry had twisted his body until he lay on his side. His legs churned slowly in the mud, now stained with crimson. He looked at Blondy, supplication screaming in his eyes.

"Damn them!" The words hissed through Kincaid's teeth.

Dru Lee moved to his side. He could feel the tremor in her body as her shoulder touched his.

"How bad is it?" she whispered.

"Bad. Damned bad. Can't you see the blood?"

"You've got to do something. You've got to help him." Desperation pinched her voice.

"Hell, yes. I'll mosey along out there and get my head blown off. That'd be a smart move."

He turned his head and looked at the girl. The droplets of moisture on her cheeks weren't rain. He wanted suddenly to take back his words, but he didn't know how to start.

They waited in silence. There was no sound from above, no indication the gunman was still watching. After a time Kincaid took up a perforated length of limb from a dead cholla, draped his slicker over it, and placed his hat atop the shaft. It wouldn't fool a man, unless that man was several hundred feet above them and looking down through a heavy mist.

Slowly, holding the slicker-draped scarecrow before him, he edged away from the protective base of the bluff. He didn't have long to wait. The instant the hat and slicker were exposed, the booming explosion of the gun sounded. The limb was jerked from his hand as the slug tore through the yellow slicker.

He turned and looked at the girl. She shook her head.

"If you just had something to reach him with. A rope. Or anything. . . ."

A rope! Blondy drove his fist into his hand. Of course!

The palomino stallion, tied to the limb of a small cedar, stood a few steps away from where McHenry had fallen. The shots had not excited the horse. Blondy had spent many an hour teaching the big horse to accept the sound of gunfire.

He felt compelled to offer her some hope.

"You've given me an idea. Maybe it'll work. If that hombre up there doesn't get smart and shoot the horse."

Softly he whistled to the stallion. The horse threw up his head at the familiar sound and eyed the man beneath the ledge. Again Blondy whistled. The palomino knew what was expected of him, and he moved toward the man. Until he reached the end of the bridle rein, still tied securely to the small tree.

"It won't work," Dru Lee breathed at his side.

"We'll see."

It took two rounds from his .45 to shoot the limb in two. The stallion didn't like the idea, but he stood fast, his ears cast forward in silent rebuke to the man he trusted.

The gunman would be wondering about those shots. Quickly Kincaid whistled again. The horse moved toward him. It seemed forever before the stallion was beneath the stone outcropping and safely out of reach of the bushwhacker's big-bore rifle.

Dru Lee had held her breath while she watched. Now she looked back toward McHenry.

"He's not moving."

Gruffly Blondy snapped, "He'll make it."

He took the lariat from the swell of the saddle and made a loop. There was little space under the stone ledge for working a rope, but the distance wasn't far. Kincaid cast the horsehair loop and began to draw it tight. It slipped from McHenry's prone figure but then tightened around one booted foot. That was enough. Hand over hand, Blondy began to pull the man toward him, leaving a trench of crimson in the rain-soaked soil.

On the cliff high above, the rifleman suddenly saw what was happening. The big rifle boomed, and boomed again. But he was firing too quickly now. The slugs slapped the mud around McHenry, and in urgent seconds Blondy had him safely shielded beneath the slanting stone wall.

Instantly Dru Lee was beside the wounded cowboy. She untied her neckerchief and used it to wipe the mud from his face. When she unbuttoned his shirt, Blondy heard her gasp. A hand flew up to cover her mouth.

"Stoke up that fire," he commanded harshly. "He needs warming up."

Blindly she obeyed.

The wound was not a pretty one. The slug, almost as big as a man's thumb, had struck the cowboy high in the left side of his chest and exited low in his back. Blood pumped from the wounds and ran among the rocks. For a moment Blondy's vision blurred. He turned his head away so the girl couldn't see.

With strips from McHenry's shirt and his own, he bound up the wounds as best he could. In brief seconds the bandages were soaked with crimson.

Suddenly McHenry groaned. His eyelids fluttered like the wings of a bird too small to fly. Then he looked up at Kincaid from where he lay on the ground. A weak smile played at the corners of his mouth.

"You tell Old Man Grimm I've decided to take the day off," he mumbled.

"Sure," said Blondy. "You just take it easy."

A lightning bolt of pain shot through the man. His body tensed against it. Beads of perspiration sprang out across his forehead.

"He got me good, pardner," he whispered between his white even teeth. "This punchin' cows is gettin' to be hell."

Dru Lee had moved back beside the wounded man. Gently she lifted his head and laid it on her knee and stroked the matted hair that lay against his forehead. McHenry looked at Blondy. One eye closed in a solemn wink.

"There's some of us who just have a way

with women. If you was to ask polite, I might give you a lesson or two."

Before Kincaid could reply, the pain came to the cowboy again. It twisted his face in an ugly mirror of agony. His knees drew up against his chest. Dru Lee looked into Kincaid's eyes, begging him to set things right. Tears drew glistening trails down her ashen cheeks.

"He can't die! He can't!" she whispered.

16

But the cowboy McHenry had used up all his time. Blondy saw him slowly begin to relax. The lines of his face softened so that he seemed to be smiling. His eyes sought out something concealed beyond the leaden skies.

The fingers of Kincaid's left hand closed on the butt of his Colt and tightened until his knuckles turned white. In a sickness of frustration, he cursed silently, calling down the wrath of the heavens on Buchanan and Grimm and the fate that had led him to this moment. And finally, with deep bitterness, he cursed himself. There was no denying it. It was Blondy Kincaid who had steered this mischievous innocent to his death.

He became aware of Dru Lee sitting with her back against the rough stone wall, her arms crossed on her chest and her hands gripping her upper arms. She was crying, her breath coming in great broken sobs. At that moment she wasn't Orlando Grimm's strong-headed daughter. She was a little girl, terrified, wretched with grief.

He spread his dirty yellow slicker gently over the face of McHenry and looked at her.

"It's not hurting him anymore."

She looked at him blankly. He moved to the fire, added some small limbs and a cow chip, and jerked his head.

"Come over here."

With trancelike movements she obeyed. She sat down beside him and drew her knees against her chest.

"I'll be all right in a minute," she said.

He reached out and put his arm across her shoulders. He felt her stiffen, but then she leaned against him, hiding her face in his chest. He could feel the slight jerking of her shoulders as she cried again.

He began to talk then, the words as much for his own sake as for hers.

"He knew what he was getting into. He knew there was bad blood between the Rafter G and Detwiler's outfit." He poked at the fire with a stick. "I can't quite figure it, though. I'd counted on the Hatchet bunch spending at least a couple of days rounding up their horses."

Dru Lee looked up.

"What do you mean?"

"That little ride I took last night was to the Hatchet headquarters."

He remembered then. The albino horse that had turned back instead of stampeding out the gate with the rest of the Hatchet remuda. One horse was all they had needed to start undoing the damage Kincaid had done. It explained that Hatchet rider sitting up there above them now, waiting to blow holes in whoever showed below. Like he had done to a good-natured cowboy named McHenry. It suddenly occurred to Kincaid that he'd never heard McHenry's first name. Now he would never hear it.

"Damn their eyes, anyhow," he said through clenched teeth.

"I'm not sure I understand what you said," Dru Lee murmured. "Why did you ride to the Detwiler ranch last night?"

"To scatter their horses. So they'd be busy elsewhere while I had a look at this patch of brush to find out what the big mystery is. It's like I figured, too. This thicket is running over with beef that should be wearing your old man's brand."

He picked up a half-burned twig and threw it into the fire.

"But I made a slight mistake. Left 'em one mount, and that was all they needed to gather in some more saddle horses."

Anger was rising in her voice.

"You ran off all their horses? It's no wonder they're wanting to shoot someone. If you hadn't done that, they might not have sent a man here. And he . . . and he might still be alive."

Wildly her eyes went to the still form of McHenry, and then, accusingly, back to him.

He wanted to snap at her, to tell her in hard words how foolish that idea was. But he could see hysteria rising to the surface again. He made his voice even.

"I think you know better than that. Those Hatchet boys don't need any extra reasons to throw down on anybody riding for the Rafter G."

He paused.

"You do remember a couple of things. They shot one horse out from under me. And jumped me while I was up on the Purgatory and nearly kicked my brains out. Just for the fun of it."

Her eyes were narrow slits, her lips drawn

to a tight line across her face.

"I remember," she said. "I remember you had Mr. Detwiler's niece at the line shack with you."

"If you'll hold still a minute, I'll explain that. I saw her get knocked off her horse by a tree limb. She was hurt pretty bad. I took her to the cabin and tried to patch her up. She was out cold the whole time."

"Oh."

She lowered her gaze, hiding her eyes from him.

"No," he went on. "This war with the Rafter G has been brewing for years. You know it better than I do. And I think you ought to face up to one thing. Your old man is as much to blame as anyone. He's too mean and hardheaded to get along with anybody."

"That's not true!" Her nostrils flared in sudden anger. "Dad may not be too neighborly, but he's never deliberately tried to hurt anyone. They've never given him a chance."

Her defense of her father was vigorous and determined. And something less than convincing. It was as though she had thought it out in her own mind a long time ago. Suddenly he felt a foolish sort of pity for this lonely daughter of Orlando Grimm. It made him light-headed. In that instant, he decided to unburden his heart. It was a decision he would regret for a long time.

"Dru Lee," he said, and the tone of his voice made her jerk her head up to look closely at him. "I'm going to tell you something. Something I never expected to say. But I owe you more honesty than you've been getting from me."

He paused and raked at the coals of the fire. He could feel her eyes on him. Already he was beginning to have doubts about the wisdom of his judgment.

"You've heard of a man named Webster Buchanan. Colonel Webster Buchanan."

"Buchanan!" The word hissed through her teeth. "A mean, heartless old man. Of course I've heard of him."

He spoke the next words very slowly.

"He's the reason I came to the Rafter G."

Bewilderment flooded her face. It was as though Blondy had suddenly become a total stranger.

"What are you saying? I don't even want to talk about him. He's the reason Dad is so bitter, so eaten up with hatred. He's the reason my mother died."

Ah, it was becoming clearer by the moment to Kincaid. The magnitude of the mistake he had made was staggering. But there was no turning back.

"I agreed to do a job for him. That's why I'm here."

Her eyes were hard on his face, as though something there held her transfixed.

"What kind of a job?"

"To ruin the Rafter G. To wipe out everything Orlando Grimm has in the world."

Had he struck her with his hand, the shock couldn't have been greater. She drew back against the face of the rock like a person recoiling from a deadly viper.

Blondy saw then he had pulled the world in on his head. His impulse to be honest and honorable had triggered calamity. There was nothing left to lose.

"I killed a man in Fort Worth. Self-defense, a fair fight. But he was Buchanan's man, and Buchanan owns the sheriff there. So I made a deal with him, to save my own skin."

If she grasped what he was saying, she gave no sign. He went on.

"Buchanan told me about his trouble with Orlando Grimm. About the feud they'd had. And about Grimm causing the death of the Buchanans' baby girl. It made Mrs. Buchanan lose her mind."

Dru Lee was shaking her head angrily from

side to side. Loathing was heavy in her voice.

"He lied! He's a horrible man, a man without a shred of decency. He hated Dad because Dad wouldn't bow down to him like all the other ranchers in the territory. He burned out Dad's pastures, poisoned waterholes, cheated him out of good grazing land, out of his best horses."

She was talking in hard, clipped tones. The words spilled out in tense bursts.

"Yes, their baby was killed. But it wasn't Dad's fault. He was riding on a ridge above the river and saw what happened. It was all her fault. Mrs. Buchanan's. She stopped the buggy and got out. Something spooked the horse, a high-spirited horse that the Colonel had practically stolen from Dad. He started to run. When the buggy went into the river, it turned over and smashed to pieces. That's when the baby was lost. Dad saw it all, from up on the ridge."

For a brief moment she put both hands over her eyes. There were tears when she took them down.

"Mrs. Buchanan claimed that Dad caused the horse to run away, and they told everyone he was the cause of the baby's death.

"My mother couldn't bear it. Couldn't stand having everyone hate her. She died right after I was born. Dad said she just didn't seem to want to live anymore."

She drew a deep, trembling breath. Her next words were flat, almost without emotion. It had all been drained out by recollections of Colonel Buchanan.

"If we . . . when we get back to the ranch, I'm going to town and talk to Sheriff Dollarhide. Try to get back the money I put up so you could get out of jail. You can leave now and go back to Texas, or wherever. Or you can stay and stand trial for killing Luke Nabours. It makes no difference to me. But when I tell Dad that you came here to ruin him—that you're doing it for Buchanan—I don't know what he'll do."

She stopped. A small cry, a whimper, escaped her throat.

"I wish you had never come! You haven't been anything except bad luck. It would suit me never to see you again!"

Blondy felt a terrible calm settle over him, the calm of complete emptiness. He had no answer to make.

Dru Lee stood up and stumbled away, and leaned with her forehead against the cold stone wall beyond the fire.

After a time Kincaid became aware that it was growing dark. Even the stingy gray light that had persisted throughout the day was fading fast. And the rain was increasing in intensity. He could hear it drumming steadily on the sodden earth and slashing through the needles of the junipers a few paces away. There was no cause to worry now about the hidden gunman.

He picked up McHenry's body, surprised at the smallness of the man, and slogged out to the cowboy's horse. He laid the body across the saddle and lashed it tight, forcing his mind to detachment. If it had been he instead of McHenry who had taken the slug, a whole heap of problems would have been solved. And Dru Lee wouldn't now be standing over there with her back to him, hating his very existence.

He shrugged into his slicker, caught up the reins of the three horses, and stood for several minutes, but he never turned around. Finally he said, "Let's go."

She was like a sleepwalker. Her face registered no emotion as she climbed into the cold, wet saddle and fell in behind the horse he was leading, the horse that was giving McHenry his last ride.

Before they had gone a dozen rods, the last light had left the sky and the grayness had become total darkness. Blondy gave the palomino stallion his head, and the two riders bent low in their saddles against the whip of rain-laden branches. When at last they came out of the valley of underbrush, he pulled the horses up and waited for Dru Lee to come alongside.

"You all right?" he asked into the blackness.

"Yes," she replied. There was no life in the word.

On they rode into the darkness, letting the horses choose their course. The rain continued to come down steadily, seeking out the openings in their slickers and washing in a bone-chilling cold. Once Kincaid pulled the stallion to a halt and reached out to put a hand on her forearm. She pulled away quickly, but not before he felt the deep tremors that racked her body.

He dismounted and stepped over to her horse.

"Get down."

She didn't move.

"Come on," he said. "You need to walk. To get the blood circulating."

He reached up and took her arm, and she slid out of the saddle like a half-filled sack of feed, barely able to stand after her feet touched the sodden earth.

Leading the horses, he held her upright and walked on into a blackness as complete as that in any mine shaft. She stumbled, and he caught her; then he stumbled and fell headlong in the unseen rocks sown along a treacherous ridge. For an instant he thought he felt her hand on his shoulder, helping him to his feet, but he couldn't be sure.

At last they climbed back into their saddles, and he heard her breathe a long, deep sigh of exhaustion. After that, time ran together.

Suddenly, out of the thickness of the rain and the starless night, a light appeared a bare fifty paces away. They were almost upon the house.

Kincaid stepped down and went to her horse. She didn't resist when he caught her in his arms. He set her on her feet and helped her up the steps to the back door.

"I'm all right," she said stiffly. He let her go on inside while he led the horses away.

At the door to the barn he unlashed the stiffened form of the cowboy McHenry, laid him gently on the straw inside, and over him spread a ragged square of canvas. Afterward, with the horses unsaddled and fed, he slogged through the downpour to the house, remembering abruptly that his head hadn't touched a pillow the previous night. No, he'd been off on a fool's mission, a nighttime ride that was worse than wasted.

Dru Lee sat at the kitchen table, her head resting on the heel of a hand. Shorty was pouring her a cup of coffee while Orlando Grimm tucked a blanket around her shoulders. It was obvious the two had been asking questions and getting little response.

When Blondy came through the door, Grimm glared at him with fire in his eyes.

"Just where in the name of tarnation have you been?" he demanded. "Had me worried sick. Afraid her horse had thrown her or stepped in a hole or gone over a cliff."

The sentence wasn't completed before Shorty broke in.

"You two wasn't supposed to be ridin' together anyhow. And where's McHenry? He lost too?"

Kincaid turned his back on the inquisitors, slid out of his slicker, and hung it with his hat beside the door. Then he dropped into a chair across the table from Dru Lee.

He skewered Shorty with a go-to-hell gaze.

"You suppose you could shut up long enough to pour me a cup of that coffee?"

Cursing under his breath, the old ramrod complied.

Grimm's face was growing strained, like a man on the verge of having a stroke. He jabbed the end of his cane against the wooden floor with a half-dozen angry strokes.

"Dammit all, boy! You come ridin' in here in the shank of the night with my daughter, her half-froze to death and scared nigh out of her wits, and set there like nothin' has happened. I want some answers. Pronto!"

Kincaid leaned back in his chair and regarded Grimm steadily.

"Tell you what," he said acidly. "I'll give you some answers after you explain one thing to me. Why in blazes have you been trying to hide that big bunch of good livestock packed into that thicket under the bluffs?"

It was as if he had backhanded the old man. Grimm fumbled with a chair, pulled it out from the table, and lowered himself gingerly. The crimson was gone from his face, leaving it an ashen gray, but he made a desperate attempt to keep the iron in his voice.

"Are you tellin' me you rode the bluffs? After I gave you strict orders to stay clear of 'em? I oughta horsewhip you, you young scalawag. Goin' off half-cocked. . . ."

Kincaid leaned forward until his face was a scant few inches from that of the old rancher.

"You're not going to horsewhip anybody,

old man. You're going to sit right there and tell me what you've got up your sleeve. And don't try to tell me you didn't know about them."

"It's none of your damn business how I run the Rafter G," Grimm shouted. "You hired on to punch cows, and that's all you're gettin' paid to do. Not to poke your nose into things that ain't none of your lookout...."

But the cold light he saw in the younger man's eyes caused him to bite off whatever else he might have said. When Kincaid spoke, the words were hardly louder than the warning snarl of a big cat.

"Those cows and calves you've got hidden away in that patch of thicket cost the life of a good cowboy today, and almost cost me mine. I figure that makes it my business."

Shorty had straightened suddenly where he stood against the cupboard.

"What did you say?"

Abruptly Dru Lee raised her head from her hand and looked at Shorty, then at Grimm.

"They killed McHenry. Someone up on the bluffs just shot him without any reason." She turned her red-rimmed eyes toward Blondy. "Or maybe they did have a reason. He rode over to Hatchet last night and drove off all their horses. He told me that."

Blondy sat tensely silent, waiting for her to go on. Was she going to go ahead and tell the old man the rest of it? That this bad-luck cowboy had come here to destroy the Rafter G?

But Dru Lee was at the breaking point. With a cry of despair, she sprang to her feet and half-ran from the room. The slam of a door echoed throughout the house.

The sound jolted Orlando Grimm to speech.

"You did what? Didn't I tell you there wasn't to be no fightin' with Detwiler's bunch? Now you've gone and done it. We won't never get our herd gathered up and trailed out. Not while we have to keep one eye on our back trail for Hatchet bushwhackers."

The flat of Kincaid's palm striking the tabletop resounded like a pistol shot.

"Didn't you hear what she said? They killed McHenry. They've tried to kill me at least twice. They've jerked down your pens and run off your cattle. And now you're apologizing for gathering cows that're running on Rafter G range. That bullet you took in the behind must have scrambled your brains."

The next words he spoke were quiet, almost gentle.

"Where are your guts, old man?"

It was the one insult Orlando Grimm couldn't abide. He rose to his feet like a raging grizzly and drew back the cane in his hand. But before he could swing it, Shorty's voice sliced through the room.

"Hold it! There's horses a-comin'."

17

It was a singular occurrence, riders coming to the ranch of Grimm. And in the dead of a cold, rainy night, too. The surly ranchman glared at Kincaid for a long moment before he lowered the cane. There was a volatile hush in the kitchen while the three men listened to the thunder of approaching hooves swelling above the drum of rain against the rooftop.

At last Grimm stirred grudgingly. He picked up the coal-oil lamp from the table and moved toward the front room. But instead of going directly to the front door, he turned aside and plucked the long-barreled Spencer from its deer-antler rack above the fireplace. By the time he reached the door, they could hear heavy footsteps on the wooden porch outside. Then an impatient fist crashed against the solid oak panel.

Grimm's anger at Kincaid was still smoldering. It showed in his movements as he drew open the door and held the lamp high to illuminate the face of the visitor there.

"What the hell do you want?" Grimm rasped. But suddenly the words were empty of the arrogant bluster they had held a few moments earlier. It might even have been fear that chilled his voice. It was not until a long time later that Blondy understood.

"We've come on business, Grimm."

Kincaid hadn't immediately recognized the face under the low-drawn hat-brim, but there was no mistaking the gravelly voice of the squat, unsmiling man who spoke. It was the law of Arrowhead and environs, Sheriff Lew Dollarhide. Behind him in the wet blackness were a half-dozen other men, their faces indistinguishable in the shadows.

For a long moment speech didn't come to Orlando Grimm. While he stood stolidly before the door with the lamp in his hand and the rifle across the crook of his arm, the sheriff grunted, "You don't have no objections to us comin' in out of the rain, I guess," and the posse moved forward into the big room and fanned out along the wall. The whisper of wet leather and water dripping from slickers were the only sounds.

At last the rancher backed up and placed

the lamp on the mantel, but the rifle remained across his arm.

Dollarhide slid his battered, rain-soaked hat to the back of his head, then deliberately opened his slicker and swung the edge of it back with his right hand until it was caught behind the walnut butt of the six-gun on his hip. It was a casual movement but there wasn't a man in the room who failed to grasp its significance.

Kincaid, just out of reach of the lamp's rays, stood a step behind Shorty and looked over the ramrod's head to the cluster of newcomers. Whatever their intentions, he didn't like the smell of it.

"I asked you what the hell you want?" Grimm repeated, but the uncertainty still lay close to the surface.

The sheriff's eyes were not fixed on the old rancher, but were moving about the big room, poking into the shadowy corners.

"And how come you brung along half the yahoos on the Hatchet payroll?" Grimm persisted.

The sheriff finally swiveled his head about and looked him in the eye.

"Because they was handy when I was gettin' up the posse."

The sheriff's cold gaze moved on, past the

door where Blondy stood half-hidden, then instantly flickered back to his face. A sudden chill whiplashed through him, but Dollarhide said nothing.

Grimm was winning his own battle with trepidation. When he spoke again, there was some of the old defiance in his tone. He shifted the long gun until one big hand clasped the breech.

"You're standin' on the Rafter G, Dollarhide. 'Less you state yore business, and pronto, I'm gonna boot yore backside out that door. You and this whole pack of riffraff that's trackin' up my floor."

His bold declaration had no visible effect on the sheriff. The lawman merely turned his gaze back to the rancher and grunted.

"Let me tell you a little story, Grimm." When the old man opened his mouth to speak, the sheriff cleaved the air with the edge of his hand, shutting off the words. "Had me a deputy once. A good man, he was, but he got itchy feet and drifted on back to Texas. Got on with the sheriff over in one of them cow towns."

"This ain't no time—" Grimm began.

The sheriff continued as though he had heard nothing.

"Got a letter from that deputy just yesterday." He tapped his breast, where the letter would be reposing. "He told me the gol'darnedest tale about an hombre he had the misfortune of arrestin' a few months back. Him and two other deputies. He said it was like tryin' to put the handcuffs on a buzz saw. One of them gents that was sworn to uphold the law spent a week in the hospital with his brains scrambled up pretty bad. And another one still can't hardly walk.

"And this deputy friend of mine developed some busted ribs and had to have an ear sewed back on. 'I ain't never seen a man that looked so easy and was so damn mean!' That's what he told me right here in this letter."

"Hell, Dollarhide. Have yore say and get it over with," snorted Grimm.

"Keep your shirt on," commanded the sheriff. "That easy-lookin' hombre they had so much fun arrestin' had outdrawed one of the top guns in them parts. And claimed the killing was self-defense. Except he had the bad luck of bein' the only survivin' witness to what happened."

It had been a gradual thing for Blondy, listening to the sheriff's emotionless recounting of some far-off happening. In another instant it came together. It was a bit of Blondy Kincaid's own history he was reciting.

The sheriff's eyes had swung back to Kincaid's face, like a compass needle hunting north. The lawman's big hand, an inch from the butt of his gun, was already in motion before the last word left his lips.

An instant later, though, a look of dismay settled on Dollarhide's seamed face. He was staring into the muzzle of Kincaid's Colt while his own weapon was still aimed in the vicinity of his right toe. It was at that moment he began thinking about giving up law work and buying that little spread he'd long had a hankering for.

Grimm, following the sheriff's stricken gaze, turned and saw the unwavering muzzle of Kincaid's .45.

"What the hell . . . ?" he blurted.

The sheriff had let his six-gun slide back into its holster. Now he nodded in Blondy's direction.

"Yeah, he's the gent I was talkin' about. Seems the sheriff over at Fort Worth made some sort of a shady deal to let him out of jail. But the murder charge is still there, as solid as the day it was filed."

"Is that right, Kincaid?" Grimm barked.

Blondy shrugged.

"You wouldn't figure the sheriff to tell a

lie, would you?"

Grimm spun back around to face the lawman again.

"Is there a reward out for him?"

Dollarhide's voice held contempt.

"I mighta knowed you'd be lookin' to make a dollar. Well, far as I know, there ain't any."

Grimm's head was thrust forward on his neck, the mien of a vulture eyeing the remains of a jackrabbit.

"You've got fifteen hundred dollars of mine that was put up to get this jasper out of jail. I want that money back."

The sheriff's voice was heavy with scorn.

"You go to hell, Grimm. Far as I can tell, he ain't exactly in custody yet."

He turned his head and sent his flinty gaze toward Kincaid.

"We gonna stand here all night and palaver while you point that six-shooter at my belly?"

Blondy had become aware of soft movement at a far corner of the big room, a corner where the rays of the lamp barely reached. He shot a glance in that direction and realized it was Dru Lee standing in the shadows, watching. This would be her final look at Blondy Kincaid, the memory she'd have to carry with her for the rest of her life. Or, more likely, for a couple of days, until she forgot he ever existed.

"Stand fast, boys," Kincaid drawled to the stout lawman and his restless posse. "I'll drill the first man that takes a deep breath."

The sudden heavy silence that followed on the heels of his words was fused with explosive tinder, but not a man stirred. There were those in the posse who had seen with their own eyes what this man's gun could do. They remembered an unfortunate devil named Luke Nabours.

Without turning his head, Blondy spoke to the Rafter G foreman, standing in frozen indecision a step away. He nodded toward the door through which the sheriff and his posse had come.

"Get out there and pick me out the best horse in the bunch. The sheriff's will do. Bring him around to the back door. After you turn the rest of 'em loose."

Shorty looked like a man anxious to obey the commands. He shouldered through the silent collection of hard-eyed men gathered at the door and went outside. Kincaid began backing toward the door of the kitchen, the barrel of his gun centered on Sheriff Dollarhide's belt buckle.

The sheriff remained in suspended motion,

his hands hanging loosely at shoulder height. His expression worried Blondy. The lawman didn't seem particularly distressed. Half a moment later he understood.

He had reached behind him to open the door that led from the kitchen to the total blackness beyond. He heard nothing except the pulsebeat of the rain against the roof until he felt a cold, hard pressure against his head, just behind his right ear. The voice that came immediately afterward sent a shock wave of dismay through him.

"Freeze, you sonofabitch!"

The words were a hiss against his ear. Kincaid froze, remembering with a wrenching sickness in his belly the last time he had heard that voice, when he lay in the grass up on the Purgatory and retched out the roots of his soul.

Now Alamo Sam reached around him and plucked the Colt from his hand. An instant later Blondy gasped as the other man jammed the barrel of his gun deep into Kincaid's side at the level of his kidney. He stumbled forward, back into the living room, where the sheriff waited with his posse. Every man was wearing a grin.

Dru Lee was there, too, but it was no smile she wore. It was an expression Kincaid hadn't seen on her face before.

"I say let's stretch the bastard's neck here and now."

The voice was that of Alamo Sam and it triggered an instant wave of assent from the half-dozen men clustered around the sheriff.

For a moment the lawman said nothing, giving his attention to the shackles he was fastening around Blondy's wrists.

"Nope," he said after a time. "We'll haul him back into Arrowhead for a proper trial. If he needs hangin' after that, there'll be plenty of time for it."

Dollarhide stepped back and looked up into the eyes of Kincaid.

"I'm going to tell you this, too, son. A while back there was a kid name of Bonney over around Lincoln who shot down a whole passel of folks, including a couple of deputies, and made a fool out of the law for quite a spell. I'm going to give you a little free advice. Don't try to pull that kind of foolishness on this here old sheriff. Not unless you're plumb fed up with livin'."

A strained silence fell across the room. It was the hush that quiets a crowd waiting for the gallows door to fall away beneath the feet of a condemned man. Then Blondy felt a weight across his shoulders. Turning, he looked into Dru Lee's eyes. She had draped his slicker around him.

"Obliged," he said.

She didn't answer, but turned and went quickly toward the door of her room.

Grimm had his mouth open, wanting to speak. But the sheriff cut him off.

"Let's head for town," said the stout lawman.

They went outside into the rain. Shorty came leading Kincaid's palomino stallion from the corral. His hands chained together, Blondy climbed awkwardly into the saddle and thought how long it had been since he had slept. He looked around at the silent cowboys swinging into their wet saddles and wondered suddenly if his head would ever again feel a pillow. This nighttime ride over the long trail to Arrowhead might never be completed for one Andrew Kincaid. Alamo Sam and his Hatchet riders would just as leave haul the prisoner into town facedown across his saddle.

But Sheriff Dollarhide was still very much in charge. "It ain't going to get any drier, gents. Move out."

The cold drizzle continued. The posse members pulled their hats down low and hunched their shoulders under their slickers. It was going to be a long night.

The sheriff rode in the lead, the prisoner beside him. Once Blondy felt another horse crowd alongside his and heard a whisper from the blackness.

"It's good and dark. Why don't you make a run for it?"

It was Alamo Sam's voice, and Kincaid heard him chuckle as he reined his horse away. It began to look less and less likely that he'd ever have the chance to settle accounts with the little Hatchet ramrod.

In the cold, wet darkness, Blondy shrugged. There would be plenty of time to worry tomorrow. He let his chin fall upon his chest and promptly went to sleep.

Daylight, sullen and gray, was making a reluctant appearance beyond the rim of mountains when the cavalcade reached Arrowhead. The cowboys who had made up the posse disappeared abruptly, seeking warmth, dryness, or a drink. It left the sheriff and Kincaid alone at the jail. His hand on Blondy's arm, Dollarhide led the way to the dark interior of the calaboose. The cell he opened was the same one which Blondy had occupied after the shoot-out with Luke Nabours.

"What happens next, Sheriff? Going to

ship me back to Fort Worth?"

The lawman turned the big key that settled the cell-door bolt into place.

"No sirree," he said. "The law right here in Arrowhead has first call on you, young feller. If there's anything left after that, them Texicans are welcome to it."

The thought was somehow amusing to him. Blondy heard him chuckle as he picked up the lamp and moved away toward the office door. Kincaid stretched out on the corn-husk mattress on the bunk against the wall and prepared to complete the *siesta* he'd begun on the ride into town.

Dollarhide came to the cell twice that day, once with a tray of breakfast and once with some news.

"You ain't gonna have to wait as long as I figured you would," he said. "Judge Bascom will be here before the week's out." A grin began to spread across his ample countenance. "Now, there's a law-and-order judge if ever I seen one. Hanged three men down at White Oakes last year for claim-jumpin', and never did even get outta bed. It was a Sunday mornin', you see."

Blondy smiled without humor.

"Yeah. He's a barrel of laughs. I can see that."

He stood up from the bunk and walked to the barred cell door.

"Sheriff, did anyone happen to mention to you that one of the Rafter G's cowboys got himself bushwhacked yesterday?"

Dollarhide didn't take him seriously.

"Why, I guess that must have slipped everybody's mind. Who might the unlucky gent have been?"

"McHenry was his name."

It turned Dollarhide around in his tracks.

"The hell you say! I've had him in my jail a dozen times. For drunkenness and raisin' general hell." He moved back and planted himself before the cell door. "I want to hear about it."

"McHenry and I were ridin' the rough country along the Piedra. Somebody picked him off from up on Lame Horse Bluffs."

"Get a look at the jasper who did it?"

"Nope. He took some shots at me, too."

"Were you on Rafter G range?"

"Yeah. Where it joins up with Detwiler's spread."

The sheriff scowled.

"Now, how the hell come Old Man Grimm didn't tell me about that last night when me and the posse were out at his place?"

Blondy finished rolling a cigarette and

reached through the bars for a match from the sheriff.

"You know the answer to that."

"Well, for the sake of argument, let's say I don't. You go ahead and enlighten me."

Kincaid exhaled a small cloud of blue smoke that enveloped the sheriff's face.

"We sort of naturally figured it was a Hatchet man that did it. And it's no particular secret that Slick Detwiler owns that badge you're wearing."

Lew Dollarhide's face grew suddenly flushed. But his eyes were hard narrow slits. Blondy thought for a moment he was going to unlock the cell door and come in.

"That's a damned rotten lie, you young renegade! Nobody owns the badge I'm wearin'. Not Slick Detwiler, not nobody! I oughta come in there and stomp your brains out. If you was to have any."

Kincaid grinned, and the lawman's face grew redder.

"It was just coincidence, I suppose, that your posse was Hatchet cowboys to a man?"

"I told you and I told Grimm. They just happened to be handy when I needed them."

Kincaid looked the sheriff squarely in the eye.

"You've got me locked up for killing one of

Detwiler's men. Now, tell me, Mr. Lawman. If it had been me that took the slug, and a Hatchet cowboy that did the killin', would you have him behind bars?"

Lew Dollarhide's jaw dropped open as though he were going to make quick answer, but then it snapped shut. A black scowl drew his heavy eyebrows together.

"Hell, yes," he said at last.

But the words lacked conviction.

18

It was midafternoon when Kincaid heard the sound of boot heels on the wooden floor outside his cell. Shorty was standing there uneasily, shifting his weight from one foot to the other.

"Well," said Blondy. "If I was a bettin' man, I'd bet a month's wages Grimm sent you to get his fifteen hundred dollars back from the sheriff."

The quick shift of Shorty's eyes told Kincaid his guess had scored a direct hit.

"That ain't none of your business, Kincaid," Shorty grunted. "I come to see you to give you this."

The hand he extended through the bars held a sack of tobacco.

"Much obliged," Blondy said. "This should last till the hangin'."

"Hell, Kincaid. It ain't nothin' to joke about," Shorty said gruffly. "When the

Hatchet get after a man, it's sure liable to be bad medicine."

"Yeah," said Kincaid. "I sort of hinted to the sheriff that I thought he might be Detwiler's man. He didn't take too kindly to the notion."

Shorty was fidgeting uncomfortably, his eyes moving nervously around the cellblock.

Blondy frowned.

"You're acting like a gent caught in somebody's hen house, Shorty. What's ailing you?"

"Well," Shorty said, "there's somethin' you maybe ought to know. Especially seein' that you're fixin' to be tried on a murder charge and all."

He took his hat off and put it back on and hitched up his trousers. Whatever it was he had to say was causing him a great deal of torment.

"If you don't spit it out, I'm going to reach through these bars and wring your scrawny neck," Kincaid growled. "Get on with it."

"Okay, okay." He cleared his throat. "You know them cows and calves you seen up there in that thicket under Lame Horse Bluffs? Where Old Man Grimm didn't want you ridin'?"

"Hell, yes, I remember. You think I'm

soft in the head?"

"They ain't part of the Rafter G herd. They sort of drifted down into that pocket from Detwiler's range."

"What are you trying to say?"

"Them's stolen cattle. Stolen from Hatchet!"

Having at last got it said, Shorty expelled a great sigh and braced himself for the onslaught.

Kincaid gripped the bars with both hands and glared at the Rafter G ramrod.

"You telling me Grimm's been rustling from Detwiler after all?"

Shorty tried to look as though it were of no consequence.

"Been doing it for years."

Blondy's eyes narrowed.

"That clears up a whole hell of a lot of things. For one, it explains why Luke Nabours and Alamo Sam kept making noises like they thought Grimm was stealing Hatchet stock. Because he was. And why that Hatchet bushwhacker sat up there on Lame Horse Bluffs and shot at everything that moved."

Shorty nodded.

"That's why we kept tellin' you to steer clear of the bluffs, Kincaid. The Hatchet outfit has suspected what was going on for a long time, but they couldn't ever catch us in the act. It was too easy. Just drift a few head of those old cows down off the mesa and into that pocket, and they'd stay there from then on."

Blondy swore quietly.

"I suppose that's what Garrett Haley was doing when he was taking those night rides. Pushing some more of Detwiler's stock down into the thicket on the Rafter G side."

Shorty grunted.

"That's right. Haley found out about the rustlin' right after he came to the Rafter G. Grimm was afraid to fire him then. And Haley got plumb greedy. He wanted to steal every piece of beef Detwiler owned."

Blondy considered the old puncher thoughtfully.

"Does Dru Lee know?"

Shorty shook his head.

"Hell, no. Grimm knows she wouldn't stand still for it."

"How long's this been going on?"

"I told you. For years. All the way back to when an old crook named Colonel Webster Buchanan owned the Hatchet outfit. But you got to understand, Kincaid. Grimm ain't been unreasonable about it. All he's done is pick up a few head now and then. Not hardly enough to notice."

"Sure. Just enough to keep his herd going after he sells off everything wearing his own brand."

He paused.

"Why did you decide to tell me all this?"

Shorty began to fidget again.

"I thought you oughta know how the cards are stacked. Arrowhead is Hatchet's town. They've been waitin' a long time to stretch somebody's neck from the Rafter G."

19

True to the sheriff's prediction, Judge Stonewall Bascom came to Arrowhead before the week expired. From his jail cell, Blondy saw him ride into town. His black frock coat, an ax handle in breadth across his shoulders, was flecked with mud. The mule he rode was a good, strong, traveling kind of mule, but the mountain trail and the judge's bulk were too much. He stood head down and spraddle-legged, unable to move after the judge dismounted.

Kincaid looked through the bars into the somber face beneath the judge's wide-brimmed hat and found no reason for optimism.

The sheriff was uncharacteristically silent when he came to Kincaid's cell the following morning. When Blondy asked for hot water and a razor, he merely grunted, went away, and came back in a few minutes with the necessary articles. He stood against the cell door and watched while Kincaid made his toilet.

"Don't look so down in the mouth, Sheriff," Blondy said. "It's not every day a man gets to enjoy a good hanging."

There was no humor in Dollarhide's face.

"If you hadn't tried to take that money pouch off of Luke Nabours after you killed him, you'd have a heap better chance of livin' to a ripe old age, Kincaid. Maybe a few years in the territorial prison. But the way it looks . . ."

He shrugged and let the sentence trail off.

"Like I told you then, Sheriff. That was my money to begin with. And it was a fair stand-up fight."

The lawman regarded him thoughtfully.

"Yeah? And who saw it?"

"Plenty of folks. The bartender. A couple of punchers. McHenry."

He stopped abruptly. The sheriff was shaking his head slowly from side to side.

"You ain't doin' so good, pardner."

At last Kincaid nodded that he was ready. Sheriff Dollarhide drew a pair of shackles from his belt.

"No need for that," said Blondy.

Dollarhide went on fastening the steel bracelets.

"Judge Bascom don't take kindly to prisoners showing up in his court without the cuffs on. And anyway, don't I seem to recall you wanting to take my horse and leave the country a few days back?"

They went out into the street, a sea of mud now from the off-and-on rains of the past week. Clouds still lay low and heavy over the semicircle of mountains that girded the town. The street was alive with people. They moved up and down the boardwalks or tiptoed with vain circumspection through the mud of Arrowhead's main thoroughfare. There was a festive air about it all.

'What's everybody doing in town?" Blondy asked. "You'd think they were planning a celebration. . . ."

The sheriff turned and regarded him wryly.

"I suppose you could call it that. It's not every day these folks are treated to a murder trial. Of a genuine gunfighter."

The meaning of it hit Blondy a moment later.

"You're barkin' up the wrong tree, Sheriff. I'm no gunfighter."

Dollarhide gazed grimly ahead.

"Tell that to Luke Nabours. And to that jasper over in Fort Worth."

The sheriff led his prisoner to the most

commodious structure in Arrowhead, the Saddle Horn Saloon. There he had to clear a path through a throng of curious citizenry gathered in a milling throng on the boardwalk outside the batwing doors.

When his eyes grew accustomed to the dimness within, Kincaid could see that the saloon was already filled to capacity. A forest of faces four deep lined the walls. Others gazed down from the second-floor balcony. Behind the long mahogany bar the burly bartender stroked his copper-hued mustache with a knuckle and put the final touches on a sign that declared: "No drinks while court is in session!"

Aligned in a row against the bar were six chairs, and in those chairs were the gentlemen of the jury. Blondy sent his gaze along the row of faces. What he saw caused his step to falter. Of the six, three were ominously familiar—faces he had seen among Sheriff Dollarhide's posse.

Kincaid spun about, prepared to register his objection to the sheriff. But the lawman was in the act of removing his hat, his reverent gaze fixed on the man behind the one table remaining in the center of the room.

Judge Stonewall Bascom was leaning back in his chair, his thumbs hooked imposingly under a pair of galluses. On the table before him lay his dust-encrusted black hat, a chain-adorned gold watch, and a water glass brimful of the Saddle Horn's finest. To be sure, drinking was prohibited in Judge Bascom's court for ordinary mortals. The judge didn't consider himself in that category.

A sudden excited murmur, the hum of an agitated bee swarm, swept through the crowd as the sheriff led his prisoner forward, and was just as suddenly choked off. Judge Bascom had raised his hand for silence. Not a man there was who dared challenge the command.

A pair of unoccupied chairs sat alone before the judge's table, and it was to those the sheriff escorted Kincaid. Every eye in the crowd followed the stout, waddling figure of the sheriff and the tall, slender cowboy with the blond hair. When they were seated, the trial began. There were no preliminaries.

"This here is the legally constituted Territory of New Mexico against one Andrew Kincaid, otherwise known as Blondy Kincaid," spoke the judge, and his deep voice rolled like thunder to the very uppermost levels of the saloon, and even to the hushed gathering on the boardwalk outside.

His Honor leaned forward, took a long sip

from the glass of whiskey on the table, and leaned back to clasp his hands across his midsection. The chair beneath him groaned in protest. He fixed the prisoner with a cold, penetrating stare, and Blondy had the sudden feeling that Bascom would know instantly if an untrue word were uttered in his courtroom.

"The charge," intoned the judge, "is murder. For the killing of one Lucas Nabours."

Slowly his glacial gaze surveyed the room, as though searching out that solitary citizen who might have the effrontery to raise objection to the accusation. At last his eyes, hidden somewhere beneath the shaggy, graying brows, came to rest on Blondy Kincaid.

"How says the prisoner? Guilty or not guilty?"

Blondy wasn't prepared for it. He had been nothing more than a spectator, as interested in the goings-on as any curious citizen of Arrowhead. Abruptly he felt the weight of every eye in the saloon on his face.

He opened his mouth to speak.

"Stand up when you address my court!" The words, properly aimed, would have driven a railroad spike.

Blondy got to his feet and took a deep breath.

"It was a fair fight, your Honor."

Judge Bascom's fist hit the tabletop before him with such force the very floor trembled beneath Blondy's feet.

"Young man, I'm going to say this once. There won't be no fooling around with my court. When I ask you a question, I don't want no long-winded speech about your opinions. I want a straight answer, and that's all!"

Suddenly Blondy Kincaid felt more alone than he'd ever felt while camped out on a mountain peak a week's ride from the nearest human being. And for the first time since he had squared off in the street against Luke Nabours, he felt a cold prickle of apprehension along his spine. This damned town and this old judge who believed he had created the universe could string him up on a new gallows and Andrew Kincaid would be dead, very dead. Fair fight or no.

Involuntarily his gaze went to the crowd, etched indistinctly in the shadows around the saloon's perimeter. But nowhere was there a friendly face. He saw the features of Alamo Sam, a half-grin stretching his thin lips into a tight line. Seated next to the Hatchet ramrod was a large gray-whiskered cowhand who peered with unseeing fixity at a point on the floor before him. Grimm's old nemesis, Slick

Detwiler, was a blind man, for all practical purposes.

In a chair at the old rancher's other elbow sat a young woman. Her hair was the color of a raven's wing, and the clothing she wore was extravagant and expensive, cut to show her ripe woman's form to full advantage. But like a single sour note in an otherwise perfect concerto, her features held an unexpected blemish. A large angry bruise covered both her eyes, a fact no amount of rice powder could conceal.

It was Slick Detwiler's niece, Alamo Sam's intended. The woman Kincaid had fetched unconscious from the depths of Purgatory Canyon.

Blondy looked long at her, but she looked away, refusing to meet his eyes.

He turned back to the judge and said, "Not guilty."

Judge Bascom's heavy thicket of eyebrows drew down until his eyes were all but hidden in the deep caverns beneath them, as though he had had a hope this matter would be settled quickly by a guilty plea and a length of Manila rope.

Now he cleared his throat and consulted a piece of paper drawn from an inside coat pocket.

"The first witness will take the stand. Claude Luther Wilbanks."

Someone in the crowd snickered, then just as quickly swallowed the sound. A man threaded his way through the spectators and stopped before the judge's table. The name had meant nothing to Blondy, but there was no mistaking its owner. It was the man they called Red, the Hatchet cowboy who had stood on the boardwalk in front of the Saddle Horn Saloon and watched Kincaid and Nabours walk out into the street.

The oath which Judge Bascom administered to the witness was brief and unintelligible. Then he nodded toward a chair beside the table, and Red sat down, nervous and ill-at-ease under the stares of a hundred pairs of eyes.

"This here defendant," said the judge, "is charged with criminally and unlawfully murderin' one Lucas Nabours. Did you see what happened on the day in question?"

Red nodded vigorously.

"I shore as hell did. Me and Luke and Witherspoon had come in the Saddle Horn for a drink. Everything was peaceable until this yahoo started in on Luke, accusin' him of stealin' his money and tryin' to bushwack him and not havin' any guts."

Red's nervousness had vanished. His voice had become more confident. He'd never before had an audience that had to shut up and listen to every word he wanted to say.

"Yessir, Judge. This Kincaid jasper was doin' his best to pick a fight, but Nabours just went on and ignored him as best he could. He told this gunfighter gent he didn't want no trouble, but he wouldn't let it lay.

"Well, Luke finally decided we'd better get on out or there'd sure enough be a shootin'. We walked outside, all three of us, and Luke said he'd go across and get our hosses. He was halfway across the street when this sidewinder came out and hollered at him."

Red looked around to ensure that his audience was paying attention. It was. The judge grunted.

"Get on with it."

"Luke turned around, thinkin' it was me or Witherspoon yellin' at him, I suppose. He saw what was happenin' and went for his gun, but he didn't have a snowball's chance, Judge. It was cold-blooded murder, sure as I'm sittin' here."

Blondy didn't stop to think about it. He sprang to his feet.

"He's lying, Judge, that's not—"

With astonishing speed, Judge Bascom's

huge hand disappeared beneath the lapel of his broadcloth coat and reappeared an instant later with a long-barreled .44 Remington. For an instant of time Blondy thought the judge might be intending to send a bullet into him. Instead, Bascom reversed the weapon and slammed the butt against the barroom table.

"Another word out of you, young man, and you'll find yourself in contempt of this here court!"

Suddenly the idea was comical. Here he was facing a date with the hangman because he'd killed a man, and the judge was threatening him with a fine, maybe, or a few days in jail. Slowly a grin spread across Kincaid's face, and Judge Stonewall Bascom began to swell like a toad filling his lungs to sound a mating call. The look he turned on Kincaid was unmistakable. He'd find a way to make this disrespectful defendant wish he'd never had a thought about smiling.

Bascom turned back to the witness.

"Anybody else see what happened?"

"Just me and Witherspoon," said Red. "Except for that drunk, McHenry. The skunk pulled a gun on us, or we'd have settled with this jasper right then."

The judge nodded and sliced the air with

his hand, waving Red down from the witness chair.

"Next witness."

The cowboy named Witherspoon sat gingerly down in the chair. He looked first at Alamo Sam and then the jury. Blondy saw one of the jurors, a Hatchet puncher, cast an almost imperceptible wink at the witness. Witherspoon relaxed, leaned back in the chair, and related precisely the same story Red had told.

When he had finished, the judge looked toward the lawman seated beside Kincaid.

"Okay, Lew."

Sheriff Lew Dollarhide tried to look tall and lean, and failed, as he strode to the witness chair. The number of votes standing around the walls of the Saddle Horn Saloon was more than enough to ensure his reelection in perpetuity.

He adjusted his gunbelt around his broad middle and cleared his throat.

"I've given these good folks my word that I'd make Arrowhead a law-abiding town, Judge. And unnecessary killin' is one of the things I swore I'd put an end to when I put on this badge. But a man can't keep out every piece of riffraff that's ridin' through the territory. I shore believe we ought to make an example of this one. Stretchin' his neck would be a sure enough good way to serve notice that this town don't intend to put up with gunslingers."

What might have been a grin pulled at the corners of Judge Bascom's mouth, and Blondy remembered the time he had ridden to a bluff overlooking the Pecos River and gazed down to see a cow that had wandered out into quicksand. Only her nose and her eyes, wild with terror, were still visible, and in seconds even those had vanished beneath the gelatinous sand. Such a feeling was oozing into the pit of his stomach.

"Now, sheriff," said Bascom gently. "This isn't the time for makin' election speeches. Just tell this court and the jury what happened when Lucas Nabours got hisself killed."

Sheriff Dollarhide shifted in the chair and drew a deep breath.

"Well, sir, I figure it happened just like those boys told it, but I've got to say I didn't see the actual shootin'. What I did see, though, was enough to make me sick to my stomach. I come up just in time to see this gunfighter gent standin' over Nabours after he'd drilled him. And what do you suppose he was doin'?"

Deliberately, his eyes drawn down to a squint, he gazed about the room and back to the judge.

"He was stealin' a money pouch from the man he'd shot! That's what he was about. If I hadn't come up when I did, he'd of got that thousand dollars off of the dead man and cut a trail for parts unknown."

"Did he offer to put up a fight when you arrested him?" Bascom inquired.

Sheriff Dollarhide grinned, an imperious sort of grin, and clasped his hands across his belly.

"He didn't dare!"

The sheriff left the witness chair reluctantly and strolled without haste back to his seat beside Kincaid.

Bascom hooked his thumbs in his suspenders again.

"Did anybody else see the gunfight, or what led up to it? Don't be bashful about speakin' up. All this here court is interested in is findin' out the true facts."

Behind the bar, still clutching the dingy bar rag in his hand, was the bartender with the copper-hued mustache.

Kincaid turned his head and looked long into the man's eyes. Abruptly the other shifted his gaze to the far wall, but a telltale wave of crimson stained his neck and washed upward to his jowls. He had heard every word Luke Nabours had spoken that day, the words that had lit the fuse that ultimately brought about the showdown.

But the bartender wasn't about to take the witness stand and tell a story that directly contradicted the testimony of the two Hatchet cowboys. He wasn't quite ready to pack up and leave Arrowhead. Or suffer a fate of greater severity.

Desperation rising in his throat again, Blondy swiveled his head and began to look through the crowd. Others had witnessed the gunfight, if not the words that led up to it. Surely there was one honest citizen in this town called Arrowhead.

His eyes fell on a face all but hidden in the press of spectators. Blondy wanted to shout. It was Dru Lee's face, somber and unsmiling, but to Kincaid it was a drowning man's straw. She might not really care if they strung up the cowboy named Andrew Kincaid, but there was consolation in the knowledge that she knew the truth of it.

The judge had been talking while Blondy's eyes were on Dru Lee and her father and Shorty the foreman. He hadn't heard the words, but now he became aware that Bascom's voice was thundering in his direction.

"Turn around and listen when I'm speakin', young man," said the judge, the words ringing cold and hard. "This here is a fair and impartial court. If you have anything to say, now's your chance to say it."

Kincaid started to get to his feet.

"Just stay where you are," the judge commanded. "There ain't no point in swearin' you in. Just get on with it."

Blondy made his voice calm and steady, and held his eyes on Bascom.

"I came to town that day to hire another hand for roundup. I figured the saloon would be as likely a place as any to find a puncher looking for work. I was sittin' about where you are, talking to the man named McHenry, when Nabours came in the door. Red and Witherspoon were with him."

The judge held up his hand.

"Hold on there. Who were you ridin' for? Who was it you were hirin' for?"

Blondy hesitated. He didn't want to say it.

"The Rafter G," he said at last. "Orlando Grimm's outfit."

There was an intake of breath from a score of throats. If he'd suddenly made confession to having smallpox, the reaction would have been the same. Most of this crowd might not know Orlando Grimm on sight, but they knew the Rafter G's reputation.

The judge nodded for him to continue. Bascom had known fully the answer to his question. He wanted to be sure everyone else in the room did.

"Nabours was standing at the bar," said Kincaid. "He called me and the Rafter G some pretty unsavory names. Names no man with any backbone would stand still for."

The judge scowled, but one eyebrow was skeptically elevated.

"You mean to tell me he just set in callin' you names before you said a word?"

"That's right, your honor. I told him we'd better settle up our accounts. So we went outside and took care of it. Fair and square."

Bascom continued to glare solemnly at Kincaid through his bushy brows.

"And how about the money pouch with the thousand dollars? I suppose you're gonna tell me it was yours all along."

Again that terrible feeling of standing in quicksand pulled at Kincaid.

"It was my money. Nabours and a partner of his had taken it—"

"Where's the partner?" interrupted the judge. "Let's hear it from him."

"He's dead."

"How come?"

"I killed him."

Judge Stonewall Bascom sent a look toward the jury, assuring himself they were listening. Then he tilted his head back and scratched at the stubble on his neck.

"Now, ain't that a pity? Seems like all the gents that could tell your side of the story are sufferin' from a terminal case of lead poisonin'. You have anything else to say?"

Blondy shook his head. His testimony had succeeded only in digging the grave deeper.

Judge Bascom built a steeple with his fingers and looked with supreme deliberation at the faces ringing the room.

"Anyone else have anything to say before I turn this case over to the jury?"

From the corner of his eye Kincaid became aware of a movement among the spectators. Every eye turned and watched as the black-haired woman seated at Slick Detwiler's elbow rose to her feet. With seeming reluctance she walked slowly forward.

Could it be? Blondy wondered. A piece of good fortune at last? He felt like springing to his feet and yelling. He had done one thing right since coming to the territory on Colonel Buchanan's fool mission. He had saved the life of this woman.

The judge was beside himself. Rarely did a pretty woman have occasion to command notice in his court. He got ponderously to his feet and executed a slight bow, succeeding only in appearing ludicrous. The raven-haired woman stopped before the table and held up a delicate hand. Judge Bascom stammered out the oath, then hurried around the table to hold the chair while she seated herself.

"And what might your name be, miss?" the judge crooned, sitting on the edge of his chair as though he were taking tea in a drawing room.

"Amanda Detwiler," said she in a voice low and soft and charged with emotion. It made Blondy's hair tingle to its very roots. There was a perceptible forward leaning of every male in the room.

"I don't know what a pretty young woman like yourself might know about a gunfighter who's fixin' to get hisself hanged for murder, but we're anxious to find out. Now, you just sit there and take your time and tell this court whatever it is that's on your mind."

He leaned forward and dropped his voice to a whisper, although the words carried to every ear in the building.

"And don't you worry none about them

black eyes, honey. Why, they're plumb fetchin'."

The judge had the look of a schoolboy in love. Kincaid thought for a moment he might break into giggles. Whatever Amanda Detwiler had to say, it was going to be gospel as far as Judge Bascom was concerned.

"I was riding through the mountains, up near the Purgatory Peaks," she said. "Something scared my horse and he bolted. I guess a limb hit me." She touched a point between her eyes with two long, fragile fingers. "It knocked me unconscious and I fell off the horse."

She nodded in Kincaid's direction.

"I guess he found me and took me to a line shack where he was camped."

Blondy suppressed a smile, an urge he hadn't previously felt. She was telling it like it happened. There was hope yet for the future of Andrew Kincaid.

But then he felt it, like a winter draft through a cabin door left unlatched. Something wasn't quite right. The woman had not met his eyes since she had taken the witness chair.

"I don't know how long I was unconscious." Tears were welling into her liquid blue eyes. "When I came to, he had taken all my clothes off. He . . . he had his hands all over me."

Her voice broke into a wail. She dropped her head and covered her eyes with her hands. Ice was flowing through Blondy's veins.

Her next words were muffled by the sobbing, but they were distinct enough to the hundreds of mesmerized ears that were straining to hear.

"I don't know what he would have done if Sam and the others hadn't shown up when they did."

20

A boiling, angry whisper swept like a whirlwind about Kincaid. Judge Stonewall Bascom sat transfixed by the words Amanda Detwiler had spoken. Now he picked up the heavy revolver and rapped it loudly against the tabletop to quiet the ground swell of talk.

"Now, now, honey," he said. "Don't you fret yourself. Everything is gonna be all right."

Then he turned his head and looked into Kincaid's face, a look spilling over with damnation. Blondy had the same sensation he'd had the day Skew's bullet creased his skull and knocked him senseless. He had been jerked into an insane nightmare.

The judge leaned forward, on his face the look of a man who was anxious to pass sentence. His eyes swept round the room and came back to rest on Kincaid's face.

"If there's one thing on this mortal earth lower than a man that'll take advantage of a woman, I don't know what it is. God gave us women to pertect and cherish and look after, seein' as they ain't strong enough to look after themselves. And along comes a gent who finds a pretty little lady knocked out of her senses and helpless as a newborn babe, and he sets in to do things . . ."

The thought was too much for Judge Bascom. Choking with passion, he could only rap the tabletop with the butt of the Remington again, although there was not a sound to disturb the stillness.

At last he took a deep breath, leaned forward, and covered the tiny hand of Amanda Detwiler with his huge fleshy fist.

"I declare this here trial closed. You gents on the jury, do your duty."

Blondy looked about him. The faces he saw registered loathing and repugnance, the kind of expression that comes to a man who looks down to see a coiled rattlesnake on the rock beside his foot. A single thought spun in maddening convolutions through his head. Would Dru Lee still believe his story, the story he'd told her when they were huddled out of sight of the bushwhacker at Lame Horse Bluffs? Or would she take this woman's word? That he was the rottenest sort of a human being.

"Judge!"

The single word, not loud but razor-edged, cut through the rising murmur. The judge, in the act of getting to his feet, froze and glared toward the speaker. Every head pivoted about.

Through the crowd came a lean, stooped cowboy, his hunched shoulders giving him the look of a man contriving to ward off blows. Then Blondy recognized him, the puncher that Alamo Sam and the Hatchet crew had left behind up there on the Purgatory, in case Kincaid had needed burying.

"I said these here proceedings are closed, mister," growled the judge with finality. "You've done missed your chance to have yore say."

Noah Rivers stood before the judge and made a visible effort to square his shoulders. It was obvious he would have preferred a nighttime stampede of raging longhorns, or at the very least a dozen wild broncs, to the task he had set himself.

"She's lyin', Judge."

Had Rivers chosen any other words with which to preface what he had to say, the judge would have ground him to humble silence and sent him on his way. But Judge Stonewall Bascom had never in his lifetime heard that particular arrangement of words. Few men of his acquaintance had the temerity to call another man a liar; none, in his memory, had ever directed such an accusation at a woman.

"My name's Noah Rivers, Judge. I was ridin' for the Hatchet when it happened. Alamo Sam and me and some of the other boys come onto the cabin where Miss Amanda was laid up. She was still out cold."

Rivers turned partially around and let his eyes settle on Alamo Sam's face.

"It looked to me like this Kincaid feller was doin' his level best to take care of her. But Alamo said he'd cook up a yarn that was sure to get Kincaid run out of the country, if not hung."

The judge spoke through his teeth.

"And what was that?"

"Why, the tale you just heard. That the defendant there had done all sorts of terrible things to the lady. Alamo had hisself a good laugh about it. But there ain't a whit of truth in what she said, your Honor, and that's a fact."

Blondy turned and looked at Alamo Sam. The Hatchet foreman was on his feet, his face the color of raw liver. His hand dipped suddenly to the holster on his hip, but just as quickly came away. Judge Bascom had forestalled such an eventuality by ordering every spectator relieved of his sidearm as he entered the premises.

Ashen-faced, Amanda Detwiler got to her feet and stumbled toward the batwing doors of the saloon. The crowd parted silently, letting her pass.

It was a time before Judge Bascom could recover his composure. At last he murmured, "Well, it don't make no difference. This here gent ain't being tried for triflin' with a woman's virtue. He's being tried for killin' a man." He took a deep breath. "Like I said, this here case is now in the hands of the jury."

He was still speaking the words when the crowd, to a man, turned to watch the progress of another individual, red-mustached, big-bellied, and a head taller than most of the men he shouldered past. It was the proprietor of the Saddle Horn, the man who had calmly invited Blondy Kincaid and Luke Nabours to take their settling of accounts out into the street.

But the judge, still smarting from the ignominy inflicted on his court by the previous witness, was bereft of patience.

"Sit down!" he commanded, slamming the butt of the revolver against the tabletop until chips of varnish flew. "This here trial is over. There ain't going to be any more testimony, and the next man that interrupts these here proceedings gets thrown in jail. You hear?"

It had been an agonizing decision for the bartender, forcing himself to the conclusion that his integrity was more precious than the business he enjoyed from the Hatchet ranch. But the decision had been made.

"Judge, I've got to have a say. I seen it. . . ."

A pulse of hope rose in Blondy's breast.

The judge lurched suddenly to his feet, swaying from side to side like a wounded grizzly.

"Sheriff, this man is in contempt of this here duly constituted court of law. I'm orderin' you to lock him up. Right now!"

The moment of hope curled blackly in Kincaid's mind, like a wisp of dry grass dropped into a flame. Dollarhide was getting to his feet when a small voice, hardly strong enough to carry the length of the room, froze him in the act.

"Your Honor. Please!"

If the voice of Amanda Detwiler had commanded attention because it was molasses-coated and tantalizing, the words spoken by Dru Lee Grimm were so much the more heeded because of their purity and innocence. In a moment there arose in the judge's being the old ache for the child his wife had never borne him.

Dru Lee came timidly forward through the press of people and stopped at the very edge of the throng, as though she feared being singled out. She kept her eyes lowered respectfully. Her voice was barely loud enough to hear, except that total silence held sway over the multitude.

"Judge Bascom," she said, "all my life I have heard people talk about you. They say that of all the judges who have ever served in the territory, you are the fairest and the wisest. Another Solomon, some have said. And did you know that many people believe you should be appointed governor of the whole territory? Because you let nothing stand between you and the truth."

She stopped, out of breath. Blondy saw that she was trembling, so shaken she had to reach out a hand to the bar's edge to steady herself. And he realized, too, that Dru Lee Grimm no more believed the words she was speaking than had Amanda Detwiler.

For Judge Stonewall Bascom, though, it

was a tribute he had long believed was his due. That it came from the lips of this sweet and guileless girl made it all the more notable and believable. What was it the Good Book said? "Out of the mouths of babes. . . ."

He sat back down and waved his hand toward Dru Lee, beckoning her forward, but she stood rooted to the floor a distance away.

"Yes, child. What is it? What is it you wanted to say?"

With her head still bowed submissively, she looked up through her lashes.

"Only that I know you want the jury to hear all the truth, your Honor. Including this man's testimony."

The judge smiled in what he took to be a Solomon-like benevolence.

"Of course, child. Of course," he said. "In my court we hear all the facts before we hang a man." He gestured toward the bartender and held his hand up, palm outward. "Do you solemnly swear . . . ?"

The bartender's name was Eichenhorst. Yes, he nodded resolutely, he had been right there behind the bar the day Luke Nabours cashed in.

"Well, now. You just go right ahead and tell us what you seen," said Judge Bascom. But he wasn't looking at the bartender. He was still gazing toward Dru Lee, now shrinking back into the wall of spectators.

"This here gent"—Eichenhorst waved a hand toward Blondy—"had come in lookin' to hire a puncher. He wasn't havin' just a whole passel of luck, either, seein' as how he was hirin' for Old Man Grimm." He chuckled, and seemed surprised that the crowd didn't join in the mirth. "In a little bit, in comes Nabours with them other two Hatchet hands."

He paused and looked through the heavy foliage of his eyebrows toward the two cowboys who had testified earlier.

"I ain't sayin' them two fellers lied to you, Judge. But what I heard sure had a different sound to it. Nabours set in to pick a fight with that yellow-haired gent there. Accused him of stealin' cows and called him some other things a man wants to be mighty careful about sayin'.

"Kincaid was stove up some, as I recollect. Still had a wrap on his shoulder. But he wasn't lookin' for a way out. He set right there as cool as you please and told Nabours he guessed it was time they settled up. And by the way, he mentioned the thousand dollars. And Luke didn't try to deny it.

"Anyways, I told 'em they weren't going

to wreck my saloon, so they drifted on outside and went at it."

The judge was leaning forward, scowling.

"Did you see what happened out in the street?"

"Yep." Eichenhorst nodded. "Stood right there in the door and watched the whole thing. And like Red and Witherspoon said, it wasn't exactly a fair fight. But they didn't tell it square. Nabours tried to get an edge on this here gent, but he was a day late and a dollar short. He should have stuck to punchin' cows."

A rumble of voices swelled through the saloon. The sharp report of the revolver butt against the tabletop failed to subdue the noise this time. Finally Judge Bascom turned the weapon about in his hand, cocked the hammer, and fired a single shot into the ceiling. When the sound of the .44-caliber explosion had died, there was no other sound. The crowd was humbled.

The judge had long ago made up his mind about the guilt of Andrew Kincaid. Changing his mind in such matters wasn't something in which he found pleasure.

"Well," he said, "It's your word agin' them two friends of the deceased. Looks like you're outnumbered."

The bartender's thick brows were drawn together into a continuous line that stretched across his broad face.

"Maybe so." He nodded thoughtfully. "But didn't Red there say Nabours was headed across the street to get their horses when the gunfight broke out? Shucks, their horses weren't across the street. They were down at the livery. You can ask ol' Jake Pepper."

The big man's words carried the ring of truth. The judge knew, and the crowd knew, it wouldn't be necessary to ask old Jake Pepper. The testimony of Wilbanks and Witherspoon had been carelessly contrived. They hadn't expected to be challenged.

Judge Bascom got slowly to his feet and for a long, tense moment glared round about him at the ring of faces. Anyone who might have an urge to question the findings of his court would need to be more than a little foolhardy.

At last he sighed, long and deeply. He needed another drink, and his glass was empty.

"I declare the charges against this defendant dismissed and wiped from the record. This here court is adjourned. Sheriff, unlock them irons and turn the man loose."

Blondy was still trying to put it all together in his head while the sheriff, refusing to meet the eyes of his ex-prisoner, unfastened the shackles.

"You can pick up yore Colt's over at the jail," he mumbled, and turned on his heel.

Of the three people Kincaid wanted words with, the first of them was nowhere in sight. Dru Lee had disappeared as soon as the bartender had begun to speak. But now that big man was in his accustomed place behind the long, shiny mahogany counter, serving drinks as fast as he could pour. If the fact that he had contradicted the testimony of a pair of Hatchet cowboys was going to hurt the Saddle Horn's business, it wasn't immediately apparent.

Kincaid moved toward the bar. The crowd of erstwhile courtroom curious gave way.

"I'm much obliged," he said, and held out his hand. It was swallowed up in the bartender's huge grip.

"I ain't too proud of myself just yet," said Eichenhorst. "Took me quite a spell to work up enough nerve. You don't owe me a thing."

Noah Rivers stood at the far end of the bar, a glass and a bottle of good whiskey before him. He and the bartender had suddenly become close friends.

Kincaid extended a hand.

"Amigo, I'm in your debt. But Alamo Sam

isn't going to take kindly to what you did."

Rivers shrugged his narrow shoulders and grinned with one side of his mouth.

"Alamo and me, we never did see eye to eye on much of anything."

He raised the shot glass, full to the brim of amber fire.

"Better have yourself a drink."

"No, thanks," said Kincaid. "I've got to locate me a young woman. And tell her I appreciate her."

Rivers winked at him over the rim of the glass.

"She's a dandy. The gent that gets a rope on her'll be mighty lucky."

Someone tugged at Blondy's elbow. He turned and found a slight Mexican youth beside him, holding out his gunbelt with the familiar Colt's settled snugly in its holster.

"Señor, the sheriff he asked me to give to you thees."

Kincaid strapped the gunbelt around his middle. Rivers chuckled.

"That sheriff had just as soon not have to look you in the eye for a few days."

The Mexican youth continued to stand nervously, shifting from one foot to the other. At last he spoke.

"Señor Reevers, there is someone outside

who wishes to speak with you. He asked me to tell you. . . ."

Blondy watched the lean, hunched cowboy follow the Mexican lad toward the batwing doors and suddenly remembered another cowboy he'd met in this same saloon, an easygoing gent who was short on temperance but long on loyalty. A fellow named McHenry.

The Saddle Horn's swinging doors were still swinging when the shot exploded in the street outside.

There was an abrupt pause among the drinkers along the bar. Then, to a man, they pivoted about and headed toward the door. But Blondy was a pace ahead of them.

The first thing he saw when he stepped outside on the boardwalk was Alamo Sam, standing with his feet planted wide apart in the mud of the street and his six-gun in his hand, the muzzle now slanting casually downward toward the fancy boots on his feet.

Kincaid turned and looked to his left, past the horse tied at the hitch rail. A man lay facedown in the mud, one hand at the butt of the still-holstered Colt's on his hip and the other curled around a fistful of soggy earth. It was Noah Rivers, the man whose testimony had sent Alamo Sam's intended stumbling away in shame from the witness stand.

Blondy was only dimly aware that Orlando Grimm and his daughter were among the score or more people who had magically gathered along the boardwalk to view the tableau of violence taking place on Arrowhead's main street. The man who owned the horse at the hitch rail was frozen in the act of untying the animal.

It was to him Kincaid directed his question.

"Did you see it?"

"Sure did," said the cowboy. "It was a fair fight. If'n you want to call it that. Alamo Sam told Rivers there that he was goin' to answer for shamin' his woman. Well, Rivers was game, all right, but he weren't no gunfighter. Alamo let him make the first move, then drew and shot him square through the middle."

He shook his head bleakly.

"Hell, he didn't have no more chance than a old woman."

He got on the horse, cast a look at the man lying in the mud, and rode on down the street.

21

Quietly, the words no louder than the voice of a man inquiring about the state of the weather, Kincaid spoke across the muddy expanse.

"Look to your gun, Alamo."

The Hatchet ramrod jerked his head about and searched the faces along the walk in front of the Saddle Horn. When his gaze reached Kincaid, his face broke into a grin.

"Well, if it ain't the mighty gunslinger! I knew I should have finished you up there on the Purgatory, Kincaid. But seein' as how you survived, I suppose now's as good a time as any to wind up that little chore."

He was reloading while he talked, and now he slid his Colt back into the holster at his hip.

"Anytime you feel lucky," said Alamo Sam.

Kincaid heard a quick intake of breath a

pace from his elbow.

"Blondy, please..."

But then Orlando Grimm was pulling his daughter to one side, out of the line of fire.

Kincaid stepped off the walk into the mud and felt the old tension in his midsection, the lightning charge of excitement dance the length of his spine. His senses were suddenly razor-edged. The air was pure and sweet in his nostrils. The mountains ringing the town stood out bold and sharp and lordly against the low pall of gray-black clouds.

He stopped in the tracks where Noah Rivers had stood and faced the Hatchet foreman. Alamo Sam wasn't looking for an edge, as Luke Nabours had. His confidence was supreme.

The crowd along the boardwalk in front of the saloon had grown to half a hundred, but the silence was clamorous. Not a breath was drawn.

Somewhere a dog barked, a single high-pitched yelp. As if by prior agreement, two hands moved.

A look of stunned disbelief passed over Alamo Sam's face at the instant the black hole appeared at the V of his shirt collar. But his reflexes continued to function for the space of a deep sigh. His finely disciplined gun hand triggered three shots.

The first of those bullets drilled into the upper end of a wooden column supporting the portico, an inch from a nest of yellow-lipped, potbellied infant sparrows. The second buried itself in the sill at the very edge of the window of the Saddle Horn Saloon, sending a fatal crack zigzagging across that priceless pane of glass.

The third struck Orlando Grimm's huge silver belt buckle, flattened itself into a ragged coin of destruction, and caromed upward into the vitals of his chest.

Blondy heard the sound and knew Alamo's shot had found a target. But he waited with his gun in his hand until the Hatchet ramrod's knees buckled and he went down into the mud.

Orlando Grimm fought to stay on his feet, but he managed only to back up three steps across the walkway. There he slid slowly down until he was sitting with his back against the wall of the saloon, the posture of a man taking his ease while he watched the comings and goings along Arrowhead's main thoroughfare.

A sharp, short cry was the only sound Dru Lee made. In an instant she was at Grimm's side, unbuttoning his shirt where the circle of new blood grew rapidly wider.

Blondy dropped to one knee beside the wounded man and saw where the two hundred and twenty grains of .45-caliber lead had ended their flight. He looked up at the semicircle of men and found Shorty standing there, ashen-faced and silent.

"Get the doc, Shorty," he snapped.

But Orlando Grimm shook his head. He started to speak, then began to cough until blood oozed from the corner of his mouth and spread into the stubble on his chin.

"Don't you go gettin' no sawbones. It'll be a waste of money."

The words had a curiously bubbling quality, as though they were being spoken under water.

The reservoir of tears Dru Lee had been holding back burst suddenly, rushing down her cheeks in a torrent. She looked into Kincaid's face, only inches from her own. Her voice trembled with grief and with bitterness.

"You! Ever since you came. You have been a plague of trouble and misery. And now you've killed him!"

Feebly Grimm raised a gnarled hand.

"No, Dru."

"But, Dad," she protested, shaking her hand. "You don't know. You don't know why he came to the ranch."

She was talking to Grimm, but her eyes never left Blondy's face.

"He is working for Colonel Webster Buchanan. He came here to ruin you!"

The old man's eyes closed and then opened. He drew a long, trembling breath, a breath that rattled deep in his chest.

"Yes, girl. It took me a while, but I finally figured that out. I knew it would happen. I've been waiting twenty years for it."

Like the shadow of a cloud moving across the sun, a frown darkened her face. She started to speak, but a sudden fit of coughing jerked the rancher's body. Flecks of blood flew from his lips and stained her sleeve.

"Dad, don't talk. Don't talk."

For an instant Grimm's voice held its old authority.

"It's time you knew, girl. I've got to say it. Or I won't rest the whole of eternity."

He sighed.

"The day the Buchanan's daughter was killed. I told you I watched it happen from up on a ridge above the river. Well, it weren't like that, Dru. It weren't like that at all. I was riding the ridge along the riverbank, all right, but when I looked down and seen that fancy buggy of the Colonel's, I just couldn't stand it. You see, the horse that was hitched to the buggy was the one I had owned. One of the finest horses in the whole territory. I had traded him to Buchanan for a matched pair of blood bays."

Pain, a pain not rooted in physical causes, showed in his eyes.

"But the Colonel had outfoxed me again. Those bays were arsenic fiends. He'd been puttin' a little tad of arsenic in their feed for a month, until they slicked up and looked like a million dollars.

"A week after the trade, I had to shoot the both of them."

He stopped talking, closed his eyes and sighed, then looked up again.

"You see how it was, don't you, girl? I just couldn't stand it anymore. I rode down the slope toward the buggy, keepin' out of sight so the Colonel's wife wouldn't see me. I didn't rightly know what I was going to do, but when I seen her stop the buggy and walk off into the bushes, I just couldn't help myself. I rode up behind that fancy rig and let out a squall, knowin' that horse was easy to spook. He took off in a dead run, headed right toward the river."

A tear spilled from his eye. It was the first time Dru Lee had ever seen him cry.

"I heard the baby squeal when the buggy took off," he said. "Then I knew what I'd done. I hadn't meant to. I only wanted to give that uppity Mrs. Buchanan a long walk home.

"When the horse and buggy went over the bank into the river, I rode after it for all I was worth. The buggy had already broke up and turned over, and I seen the child in the water. A little tyke, no bigger than a minute. I swung down and got aholt of that frilly little pink dress."

He closed his eyes. For a moment Blondy feared he had used up all his strength. But he began talking again.

"Well, I knowed Mrs. Buchanan hadn't got a good look at me or my horse. All she'd heard was me whoopin' and hollerin'. But there wasn't no way I could take that baby back to her without admittin' what I'd done. That would've meant a horsewhippin' by the Colonel. And probably gettin' my neck stretched from a tree. He'd-a done it, too."

He squeezed Dru Lee's hand weakly.

"Honey, you can see how it was, cain't you? I got home and tried to tell the missus, but she wouldn't have none of it. She threw a fit, tellin' me I had to take the baby back to the Buchanans. I didn't mean to hurt her, but she wouldn't shut up. Just kept on yellin' at me. She hit her head against the stove when she fell, but I weren't payin' no mind.

"When I come back in the house, she was dyin'. And that little baby was a-lyin' there on the bed beside her, its little eyes a-lookin' up at me and sheddin' nary a tear."

Dru Lee still had not comprehended, and Grimm looked into her face with the eyes of a man consigning a beloved child to death.

"Nobody ever knew that little baby didn't die in the river. Nobody ever knew that Old Man Grimm took her and raised her as his very own!"

The only sound that came to Blondy's ears was the rattle of Grimm's breathing. Dru Lee knelt beside him in stunned, stricken silence, her face the pallor of one confined too long to a sickroom. How long would it take, Blondy wondered, before she would accept the fact that she was not the daughter of Orlando Grimm, but the progeny of Webster Buchanan, a name she had spent a lifetime loathing.

Grimm had got it said, and in the saying had gained a measure of peace. Kincaid could see that in his face. But the old man wasn't through. Not quite. With a hand growing increasingly feeble, he reached and caught Blondy's arm.

"Them cows and calves you seen in the

trap up at Lame Horse Bluffs? Your suspicions was correct, son. It started back when Buchanan owned the Hatchet. Every now and then I'd haze a few head of the Colonel's stock down off the mesa into that trap under the bluffs. Why, them old cows wouldn't leave that good grass and cover for love n'r money."

"I know," said Kincaid. "Shorty told me."

Grimm went on as though he hadn't heard, but he was talking now to the girl.

"Don't you see? Buchanan owed it to me. He'd skinned me at every turn, beat me in every trade. I was just takin' back what was rightfully mine." He closed his eyes. "It was so easy, I guess I just never did see any reason to stop."

A frothy crimson bubble appeared at the corner of his mouth. His breathing quickened. When he opened his eyes again, Blondy could see the agony, and another, darker shadow lurking there.

"Dru Lee, honey," he said, and they had to lean closer to hear the words. "You'll forgive an old man, won't you? I didn't mean no real harm. I didn't know that little baby was in the buggy. I swear I didn't."

He was crying. Tears welled from his eyes and washed down his cheeks, mixing with the blood on his chin.

"It's all right, Dad," she whispered, but the last word sounded hollow to Blondy's ears.

She put her arm around the old man's neck and pulled his head to her breast, but Orlando Grimm had died with the tears still spilling down his face.

The crowd was breaking up, the citizens of Arrowhead drifting away in grim silence. They had seen enough violence and death for one day.

Blondy stood and moved a pace away, looking down at the girl cradling a stranger's head in her arms.

"I've got to go send a wire," he said gently.

She looked up, her eyes red-rimmed but dry. She had no more tears.

"What?"

"I've got to send a wire. To Fort Worth. To Buchanan."

She drew a deep breath.

"Are you going to tell him? About me?"

"Do you want me to?"

"No!" The word was brittle, raw-edged. But Blondy could see there was something else. A moment later she said softly, "Not now. Not yet."

He turned to walk away, but her voice stopped him. He turned about, aware that the rain had started again. An intermittent necklace of raindrops slid down a rafter of the portico and began a soft patter against her shoulder. She didn't seem to notice.

"What will you do?"

She had intended the words to be indifferent, but they came out too quickly.

"I don't know." He shrugged. "I hadn't thought about it."

He had the feeling she was holding her breath.

"Do you think . . . do you think you could stay on at the Rafter G? Just for a little while? Until things get sort of straightened out?"

Kincaid looked beyond her to the muddy street, where a half-dozen men were gathering up the bodies of two cowboys. His gaze came back to Dru Lee and the man lying dead against her knee. She was right. Blondy Kincaid had brought nothing but misfortune, a pestilence of misery and sorrow, into her life.

He shook his head.

"Give me a little time. I'll have to think about it."

He went on down the boardwalk toward the telegraph office. He looked back once and saw that she hadn't moved. The droplets of rain were still falling against her shoulder, soaking the ends of her short brown hair and the man's shirt she wore. It occurred to him he had never seen her in anything but shirt and trousers. He wondered how she'd look in a dress. A pink one, maybe, with frills.

The publishers hope that this
Large Print Book has brought
you pleasurable reading.
Each title is designed to make
the text as easy to see as possible.
G. K. Hall Large Print Books are
available from your library and
your local bookstore. Or you can
receive information on upcoming
and current Large Print Books by
mail and order directly from the
publisher. Just send your name
and address to:

G. K. Hall & Co.
70 Lincoln Street
Boston, Mass. 02111

or call, toll-free:

1-800-343-2806

A note on the text
Large print edition designed by
Fred Welden.
Composed in 18 pt Times Roman
on a Mergenthaler 202
by Compset Inc., Beverly MA.

Yours to Keep
Withdrawn/ABCL